Love and Friendship

Love and Friendship

Jane Austen

ET REMOTISSIMA PROPE

Hesperus Classics

Hesperus Classics
Published by Hesperus Press Limited
4 Rickett Street, London sw6 1ru
www.hesperuspress.com

Love and Friendship first published in 1922
The Three Sisters first published in 1933
A Collection of Letters first published in 1922

First published by Hesperus Press Limited, 2003
Reprinted 2004, 2006

Foreword © Fay Weldon, 2003

Designed and typeset by Fraser Muggeridge
Printed in Jordan by Jordan National Press

isbn: 1-84391-060-8

CONTENTS

FOREWORD

What a delightful volume this is – Jane Austen on the lives and loves of teenage girls, in two short epistolary novels and five brilliant short stories written in letter form, and so hitherto neglected. And whatever's changed in the last two hundred years? These are the same young girls we know today – monsters of hypocrisy while doing their best to be good – moaning, accusing, forgiving, giggling, weeping, fainting, screaming in delight or outrage, who's to tell; one moment seducing, the next spurning; kind and cruel by turns, intuitive yet obtuse; wholly resistant to parental advice, hopelessly noisy, and in general able to charm and appal within the hour. These days they use mobile phones the better to live in a flurry of excitement: two centuries back they had to content themselves with writing letters. (Mind you, a letter sent one day got there the next: those were the days!)

Jane Austen wrote the works in this book when she herself was in her teens, fresh to the task of writing fiction. She recorded the fitful and whimsical awfulness of her contemporaries with the same exquisite intelligence, mirthful good humour and elegance of style as when she was writing the five great novels of her twenties and thirties. An education in the classics, which she was fortunate enough to have – her clergyman father taught her Latin and Greek – was still fresh in her mind; the rhythm of the prose falls naturally into cadences of three. 'I hope you like my determination; I can think of nothing better; and am your ever affectionate – Mary Stanhope,' writes her wilful heroine in *The Three Sisters*. (See, it's infectious. What did I just write? – 'exquisite intelligence, mirthful good humour and elegance of style'. Always the cadence of three, as a chord resolves.) If all within is in letter form, perhaps it's because (like texting today) the letter comes so naturally to the young, along with, in Austen's case, the pure joy – nothing purer – of invention. This is exhilarating, energising writing: the writer seems in love with her new-found ability. The reader laughs aloud, and yet feels a kind of melancholy for the loss of youth and if not exactly innocence – for these young heroines of Austen's are far from innocent – then the bravado, courage and hope that go with being young and silly. As we read, the sense of our lives as a continuous stream from then to now is very strong indeed. Austen is trapped in these pages as a girl, but we know her to have died young, and that is sad.

Austen's early works tend to be dismissed as juvenilia: they should not be. True, she was certainly very young, fourteen when, in 1790, she wrote *Love and Freindship*, kindly corrected by the posthumous publishers to '*Friendship*', but I believe 'Freindship' has its own charm and who is to say it was not a deliberate mistake, since Laura, its heroine, was the one writing the letters? One imagines the teenage Jane Austen sitting there by the fire, reading aloud to her family, as was her custom; they will have cut her down to size with gentle mockery, no doubt, rather as she tends to do with her own characters. As you are done by, so you do. 'Jane,' perhaps they will have said, 'really, you can't have quite so much swooning away in a book, it's too absurd, even though your friends may have a tendency to it in real life. And perhaps it is not quite the kind of thing you should be writing – best to write about what you know, surely. Not this rather wild invention. You don't find this kind of thing in serious books, only in trash, which to our minds you read too much of anyway. And look here, you've spelled friendship wrong. It's i before e except after c…' and Jane will have retreated, hurt, to fight again another day.

But to my mind there is very little juvenile about these early works other than their subject matter and the odd spelling mistake at a time when spelling was not yet so highly regularised as it is today. The prescience of an early death seemed to hothouse the writers of her generation, as it did her. There was little time to practise. You got it right first time round. Death could come early.

Of her more or less coevals, Shelley died at the age of thirty, in 1822, leaving a great body of work behind him. (His child bride Mary began work on *Frankenstein* when she was eighteen, and no one could describe that monster work as juvenilia.) Byron died at the age of thirty-six, in 1824. Keats at the age of twenty-six, in 1821. Jane Austen, born in 1775, made it to forty-one – doing rather better than the rest of them, but then she lived more quietly, without drink, drugs or wild spouse.

The novella *Love and Friendship* is a romp through an episode of runaway teenage life. It is said to be a burlesque of Richardson's epistolary novels *Pamela, Clarissa*, and *Sir Charles Grandison*, but these were written some forty years before Austen began the oeuvre of her fifteenth year. I have no doubt she had read enough contemporary kitchen-table novels by that time to get her going without recourse to Richardson. Kitchen-table novels, so called because they were seen as fit only for servant girls – these days I suppose we could call it kitch-lit – were not so very different from our chick-lit. Our version is designed to be read, not in someone else's kitchen in the few precious hours off, but on public transport on the way to the office, or on holiday in the sun: it serves the same purpose all the same: it fills the head with dreams of love.

Kitch-lit uses Gothic backgrounds, castles and mists and

lonely cottages on the moor – who knows what danger lurks within, but still the heroine ventures out – and the underlying fear is more real. It is of starvation, abduction, false marriage and ravishment. Chick-lit uses loft spaces and family homes as background, and the fear is of social humiliation, sexual harassment behind the filing cabinet, or Rohypnol at the wine bar: the hope is the same – of marriage and happiness ever after.

Pride and Prejudice, written in 1822 – women's favourite novel of all time, according to a recent BBC poll – and normally listed amongst the five major Austen novels, remains to my mind kitch-lit: it's a simple romance, poor-girl Elizabeth gets rich-boy Darcy in the most unlikely fashion. But the plot is not the point. It is the lively use of language, the sense of the keen, desperate intelligence, already to be found in the earlier *Love and Friendship*, which so delights – added of course to the brilliance and familiarity of the subsidiary characters. We all know a living Mr Bennett, a Mr Collins, a Lady de Burgh, only too well – just as, as children, we knew all too well their animal equivalents in the books we loved, *The House at Pooh Corner, Wind in the Willows, Alice in Wonderland* – Eeyore, Tigger, Badger, Toad, White Rabbit and the Dormouse – all alive and well and living around the corner. It is precisely because so little changes when it comes to human nature, and those who can delineate it in fiction are so rare, that books from the past remain relevant, loved, read and reread over the centuries. Jane Austen's original readers might have read by candle and lamplight, their successors by gaslight, and we in the brilliance of halogen, but her text remains the same and we are in fellowship with the past when we read.

That wicked, thieving, unscrupulous and forever fainting pair, Laura and Sophia, in *Love and Friendship* are a glorious invention. They fainted to the great detriment of their health, of course: in Sophia's last words to Laura she beseeches her friend to beware of fainting fits: 'Though at the time they may be refreshing and agreeable, yet believe me, they will, in the end, if too often repeated and at improper seasons, prove destructive to your constitution.' Fainting among girls may not be as fashionable as once it was, these being the days of women's empowerment, but I remember a time when there was an epidemic of it at my own girls' high-school, and re-freshing and agreeable fainting was, I recall, just as Austen describes it – the swoony blacking-out, the helplessness, the crumpling – most sensuous. More and more girls each day had to be dragged out unconscious, to recover presently, without apparent ill effects, once in the fresh air. Local health officers were brought in, parents panicked, the school was about to close. Then the headmistress lost her temper and said to all assembled: 'Any girl who faints will get a detention,' and the outbreak stopped as quickly as it began. But this is by the way.

It is supposed that *Northanger Abbey*, published post-humously in 1817, was the book Austen worked on after finishing with *Love and Friendship*, though no one can of course be sure. It is certain that by the time Jane Austen had finished it – there was more to her life than writing, as her letters to her sister Cassandra attest; there were balls to go to, bonnets to buy and trim, friends and family to visit, she couldn't be always writing (what was it someone said to the historian Edward Gibbon of that massive work *The Decline and Fall of the Roman Empire*, 'Still scribbling away, Mr Gibbon?') – our new heroine has grown up, cleaned up her act, keeps good company, never faints, and though still hope-lessly influenced by bad novels, is practically as respectable a girl as Bridget Jones.

Jane Austen was, alas, always being advised to 'write about what she knew'. Men were encouraged to invent, not so women. Who knew into what alarming and indecent lands of fantasy the female novelist might not wander, if left unchecked? A reviewer of *Northanger Abbey* wrote complaining that General Tilney seemed to have been drawn from the imagination, 'for it is not a very probable character, and is not portrayed with our authoress' usual taste and judgement'. A matter of taste, then. And another critic wrote, 'This is the forte of our authoress: as soon as ever she leaves the shores of her own experience, and attempts to delineate fancy characters she falls at once to the level of mere ordinary novelists. Her merit consists altogether in her remarkable talent for observation' – and then goes on to complain about Austen's want of imagination! I fear Jane Austen took this kind of comment too much to heart. Her fancy wanders widely enough in *Love and Friendship*, the early *Lady Susan*, and to a smaller degree in *Northanger Abbey*. But had she *not* listened, *not* drawn back, *not* restricted herself to what she knew, or had she lived in the same social milieu as the Shelley set, say, or run off with a toy boy, Lord Byron, and so known more, what might she not have written? The Prince Regent, an admirer of Ms Austen's work, and perhaps not realising quite what a satirist she was, wanted her to write for him 'a historical romance based on the House of Saxe-Coburg', but she politely replied that though 'it might be more to the purpose of profit and popularity than such pictures of domestic life in country villages as I deal in, I could no more write a romance than an epic poem.' I do rather wish she had said yes, not no. It would have got her out and about more. I know this is heresy; Jane Austen is the darling of the quiet and retiring everywhere. But she might even have met a charming prince in the course of her researches. (And that's even a worse heresy, for who is to say that the single woman has a worse time of it than a wife?) And we must of course be grateful for what we have: that her father consented to send *Pride and Prejudice* to Mr Thomas Egerton the publisher, who rather reluctantly agreed to publish it (a Mr Cadell having earlier turned it down), and that sister Cassandra did not burn the manuscript of *Northanger Abbey* and the juvenilia, as she did so many of Jane's letters.

The five fictional letters in this volume, very much ignored by critics to date, turn out to be a collection of five just about perfect short stories, true to the classic form, punchlines and all. In the brief *From a Young Lady Rather Impertinent to Her Friend* the story ends so neatly and with such a graceful bathos: 'This was an answer I did not expect – I was quite silenced, and never felt so awkward in my life.' The more remarkable that they are practically the first of their kind, written by the young Austen at a time when the short story scarcely existed at all. The 'short story' did not begin to appear until the middle of the nineteenth century, when Walter Scott got going, and, in America, Washington Irvine, Hawthorne and Edgar Allan Poe, and, in Germany, Goethe and Meyer. And here we have Jane Austen, not yet seventeen, quietly getting on with the new form from first principles. Of course there was Chaucer and his *Canterbury Tales*, centuries before – there is nothing entirely new under the sun – but those rude verses were hardly Austen territory. She did it by instinct – writing in letter form because that's all she'd done to date: you can say a great deal in a very short space of time. Let's try it: set up your characters, set the scene, make your point and get out, she'd have thought, sitting up in bed one morning. Something halfway between a poem and a novel.

Or, as Edgar Allan Poe defined it in 1842, rather more elaborately, and having perhaps imagined that he had discovered the form – 'a short story is a prose narrative requiring anything from half an hour or one or two hours in perusal: a story that concentrates upon a unique and single effect and one in which the quality of effect is the main objective. In the end the form has shown itself to be so flexible and susceptible of so much variety that its possibilities seem almost endless.'

Your foreword writer has a collection or so of short stories to her name, but must admit that once when teaching Creative Writing – that unteachable subject – at the Sydney Institute of Technology (and what an astonishingly bright lot of students they were, knowing much more about the theory of writing than I ever did) they complained that mine were not short stories at all, were not true to the form as they had been taught it, and I had no business thus describing them. I should have quoted Edgar Allan Poe at them – 'its possibilities are endless' – and not have just said crossly that so far as I was concerned a short story was a story that stopped in a short time. Adding to annoy, what's more, that a poem was simply prose that never got to the end of the page. But I digress.

Also in the letters, besides the perfect punchlines, are the embryonic form of later novels – Lady Greville in *Letter the Third, from a Young Lady in Distressed Circumstances* is an early sketch of Lady Catherine de Burgh in *Pride and Prejudice*. In *Letter the First, from a Mother to Her Friend*, here's poor vulgar Mrs Bennett, that much put-upon lady (I speak as one who frequently has the vapours). Alas, what Jane Austen had Mrs Bennett forecast for her daughters if they didn't marry, and was laughed at for her pains, came true for the Austen daughters: the Revd Austen dies, the house is entailed away, the little family of women are left homeless and penniless, and are obliged to live by the grace and favour of relatives. I daresay Jane Austen saw the irony in this, and found it painful.

In the meantime I fall about with delight at the sheer wickedness of what's contained in this volume. Laura, in *Love and Friendship*, writing to Marianne, at Marianne's mother's behest – 'Our neighbourhood was small, for it consisted only of your mother.' I don't know why that collapses me with mirth, but it does. It's so cunningly vengeful. Perhaps, one thinks, it's the way the calmly and contentedly formal interacts with the desperation of living with screaming rural dullness, which gives the writing its needling twists, its amused, defiant energy.

Or this from *The Three Sisters*, when Sophy threatens to tell the world that she will speak very ill of Mr Watts if he proposes to her sister, and her mother replies, 'Mr Watts has been too long abused by all the world to mind it now.' Or that elegant, delightful use of petulant bathos that Austen's so good at – from the now tragic Laura in *Love and Friendship*: 'My accomplishments too begin to fade – I can neither sing so well nor dance so gracefully as I once did – and I have entirely forgotten the Minuet Dela Cour.' Or the Wildean bon mots which so abundantly litter the text: 'When there is so much love on one side, there is no occasion for it on the other.' You take your pick – and enjoy.

– Fay Weldon, 2003

Love and Friendship

Deceived in Friendship and Betrayed in Love

To Madame La Comtesse de Feuillide[1],
this novel is inscribed by her obliged humble servant,
the author

Letter The First
From Isabel to Laura

How often, in answer to my repeated entreaties that you would give my daughter a regular detail of the misfortunes and adventures of your life, have you said: 'No, my friend, never will I comply with your request till I may be no longer in danger of again experiencing such dreadful ones.'

Surely that time is now at hand. You are this day fifty-five. If a woman may ever be said to be in safety from the determined perseverance of disagreeable lovers and the cruel persecutions of obstinate fathers, surely it must be at such a time of life.

Isabel

Letter The Second
Laura to Isabel

Although I cannot agree with you in supposing that I shall never again be exposed to misfortunes as unmerited as those I have already experienced, yet to avoid the imputation of obstinacy or ill nature, I will gratify the curiosity of your daughter; and may the fortitude with which I have suffered the many afflictions of my past life prove to her a useful lesson for the support of those which may befall her in her own.

Laura

Letter The Third
Laura to Marianne

As the daughter of my most intimate friend, I think you entitled to that knowledge of my unhappy story which your mother has so often solicited me to give you.

My father was a native of Ireland and an inhabitant of Wales; my mother was the natural daughter of a Scotch peer by an Italian opera-girl – I was born in Spain, and received my education at a convent in France.

When I had reached my eighteenth year I was recalled by my parents to my paternal roof in Wales. Our mansion was situated in one of the most romantic parts of the Vale of Usk. Though my charms are now considerably softened and somewhat impaired by the misfortunes I have undergone, I was once beautiful. But lovely as I was, the graces of my person were the least of my perfections. Of every accomplishment accustomary to my sex, I was mistress. When in the convent, my progress had always exceeded my instructions, my acquirements had been wonderful for my age, and I had shortly surpassed my masters.

In my mind, every virtue that could adorn it was centred; it was the rendezvous of every good quality and of every noble sentiment.

A sensibility too tremblingly alive to every affliction of my friends, my acquaintance, and particularly to every affliction of my own, was my only fault, if a fault it could be called. Alas! how altered now! Though indeed my own misfortunes do not make less impression on me than they ever did, yet now I never feel for those of another. My accomplishments too begin to fade – I can neither sing so well nor dance so gracefully as I once did – and I have entirely forgotten the Minuet Dela Cour.

Adieu,

Laura

LETTER THE FOURTH
Laura to Marianne

Our neighbourhood was small, for it consisted only of your mother. She may probably have already told you that, being left by her parents in indigent circumstances, she had retired into Wales on economical motives. There it was our friendship first commenced. Isabel was then one and twenty. Though pleasing both in her person and manners, between ourselves she never possessed the hundredth part of my beauty or accomplishments. Isabel had seen the world. She had passed two years at one of the first boarding-schools in London, had spent a fortnight in Bath, and had supped one night in Southampton.

'Beware, my Laura,' she would often say. 'Beware of the insipid vanities and idle dissipations of the metropolis of England; beware of the unmeaning luxuries of Bath, and of the stinking fish of Southampton.'

'Alas!' exclaimed I. 'How am I to avoid those evils I shall never be exposed to? What probability is there of my ever tasting the dissipations of London, the luxuries of Bath, or the stinking fish of Southampton? I who am doomed to waste my days of youth and beauty in a humble cottage in the Vale of Usk.'

Ah! little did I then think I was ordained so soon to quit that humble cottage for the deceitful pleasures of the world.

Adieu,

Laura

Letter The Fifth
Laura to Marianne

One evening in December as my father, my mother and myself were arranged in social converse round our fireside, we were of a sudden greatly astonished by hearing a violent knocking on the outward door of our rustic cottage.

My father started – 'What noise is that?' said he.

'It sounds like a loud rapping at the door,' replied my mother.

'It does indeed,' cried I.

'I am of your opinion,' said my father. 'It certainly does appear to proceed from some uncommon violence exerted against our unoffending door.'

'Yes,' exclaimed I. 'I cannot help thinking it must be somebody who knocks for admittance.'

'That is another point,' replied he. 'We must not pretend to determine on what motive the person may knock – though that someone *does* rap at the door, I am partly convinced.'

Here, a second tremendous rap interrupted my father in his speech, and somewhat alarmed my mother and me.

'Had we better not go and see who it is?' said she. 'The servants are out.'

'I think we had,' replied I.

'Certainly,' added my father, 'by all means.'

'Shall we go now?' said my mother.

'The sooner the better,' answered he.

'Oh! let no time be lost,' cried I.

A third more violent rap than ever again assaulted our ears.

'I am certain there is somebody knocking at the door,' said my mother.

'I think there must,' replied my father.

'I fancy the servants are returned,' said I. 'I think I hear Mary going to the door.'

'I'm glad of it,' cried my father, 'for I long to know who it is.'

I was right in my conjecture for Mary, instantly entering the room, informed us that a young gentleman and his servant were at the door, who had lost their way, were very cold, and begged leave to warm themselves by our fire.

'Won't you admit them?' said I.

'You have no objection, my dear?' said my father.

'None in the world,' replied my mother.

Mary, without waiting for any further commands, immediately left the room and quickly returned, introducing the most beauteous and amiable youth I had ever beheld. The servant she kept to herself.

My natural sensibility had already been greatly affected by the sufferings of the unfortunate stranger, and no sooner did I first behold him than I felt that on him the happiness or misery of my future life must depend.

Adieu,

Laura

LETTER THE SIXTH
Laura to Marianne

The noble youth informed us that his name was Lindsay – for particular reasons, however, I shall conceal it under that of Talbot. He told us that he was the son of an English baronet, that his mother had been for many years no more, and that he had a sister of the middle size.

'My father,' he continued, 'is a mean and mercenary wretch – it is only to such particular friends as this dear party that I would thus betray his failings. Your virtues, my amiable

Polydore[2],' – addressing himself to my father – 'yours, dear Claudia, and yours, my charming Laura, call on me to repose in you my confidence.'

We bowed.

'My father, seduced by the false glare of fortune and the deluding pomp of title, insisted on my giving my hand to Lady Dorothea. "No, never!" exclaimed I. "Lady Dorothea is lovely and engaging – I prefer no woman to her – but know, sir, that I scorn to marry her in compliance with your wishes. No! Never shall it be said that I obliged my father." '

We all admired the noble manliness of his reply. He continued:

'Sir Edward was surprised; he had perhaps little expected to meet with so spirited an opposition to his will. "Where, Edward, in the name of wonder," said he, "did you pick up this unmeaning gibberish? You have been studying novels I suspect." I scorned to answer: it would have been beneath my dignity. I mounted my horse and, followed by my faithful William, set forth for my aunt's.

'My father's house is situated in Bedfordshire, my aunt's in Middlesex, and though I flatter myself with being a tolerable proficient in geography, I know not how it happened, but I found myself entering this beautiful vale which I find is in South Wales, when I had expected to have reached my aunt's.

'After having wandered some time on the banks of the Usk without knowing which way to go, I began to lament my cruel destiny in the bitterest and most pathetic manner. It was now perfectly dark, not a single star was there to direct my steps, and I know not what might have befallen me had I not at length discerned through the solemn gloom that surrounded me a distant light, which as I approached it, I discovered to be the cheerful blaze of your fire. Impelled by the combination of misfortunes under which I laboured, namely fear, cold and hunger, I hesitated not to ask admittance which, at length, I have gained. And now, my adorable Laura,' continued he, taking my hand, 'when may I hope to receive that reward of all the painful sufferings I have undergone during the course of my attachment to you, to which I have ever aspired. Oh! when will you reward me with yourself?'

'This instant, dear and amiable Edward,' replied I. We were immediately united by my father who, though he had never taken orders, had been bred to the Church.

Adieu,

Laura

LETTER THE SEVENTH
Laura to Marianne

We remained but a few days after our marriage in the Vale of Usk. After taking an affecting farewell of my father, my mother and my Isabel, I accompanied Edward to his aunt's in Middlesex. Philippa received us both with every expression of affectionate love. My arrival was indeed a most agreeable surprise to her as she had not only been totally ignorant of my marriage with her nephew, but had never even had the slightest idea of there being such a person in the world.

Augusta, the sister of Edward, was on a visit to her when we arrived. I found her exactly what her brother had described her to be – of the middle size. She received me with equal surprise, though not with equal cordiality, as Philippa. There was a disagreeable coldness and forbidding reserve in her reception of me which was equally distressing and unexpected: none of that interesting sensibility or amiable sympathy in her manners and address to me when we first met which should have distinguished our introduction to each other. Her language was neither warm, nor affectionate, her expressions of regard were neither animated nor cordial; her arms were not opened to receive me to her heart, though my own were extended to press her to mine.

A short conversation between Augusta and her brother, which I accidentally overheard, increased my dislike of her and convinced me that her heart was no more formed for the soft ties of love than for the endearing intercourse of friendship.

'But do you think that my father will ever be reconciled to this imprudent connection?' said Augusta.

'Augusta,' replied the noble youth, 'I thought you had a better opinion of me than to imagine I would so abjectly degrade myself as to consider my father's concurrence in any of my affairs either of consequence or concern to me. Tell me, Augusta, with sincerity: did you ever know me consult his inclinations or follow his advice in the least trifling particular since the age of fifteen?'

'Edward,' replied she, 'you are surely too diffident in your own praise. Since you were fifteen only! My dear brother, since you were five years old, I entirely acquit you of ever having willingly contributed to the satisfaction of your father. But still I am not without apprehension of your being shortly obliged to degrade yourself in your own eyes by seeking a support for your wife in the generosity of Sir Edward.'

'Never, never, Augusta, will I so demean myself,' said Edward. 'Support! What support will Laura want which she can receive from him?'

'Only those very insignificant ones of victuals and drink,' answered she.

'Victuals and drink!' replied my husband, in a most nobly

contemptuous manner. 'And dost thou then imagine that there is no other support for an exalted mind (such as is my Laura's), than the mean and indelicate employment of eating and drinking?'

'None that I know of, so efficacious,' returned Augusta.

'And did you then never feel the pleasing pangs of love, Augusta?' replied my Edward. 'Does it appear impossible to your vile and corrupted palate to exist on love? Can you not conceive the luxury of living in every distress that poverty can inflict, with the object of your tenderest affection?'

'You are too ridiculous,' said Augusta, 'to argue with; perhaps however you may in time be convinced that –'

Here I was prevented from hearing the remainder of her speech by the appearance of a very handsome young woman who was ushered into the room at the door of which I had been listening. On hearing her announced by the name of Lady Dorothea, I instantly quitted my post and followed her into the parlour, for I well remembered that she was the lady proposed as a wife for my Edward by the cruel and unrelenting baronet.

Although Lady Dorothea's visit was nominally to Philippa and Augusta, yet I have some reason to imagine that, acquainted with the marriage and arrival of Edward, to see me was a principal motive to it.

I soon perceived that though lovely and elegant in her person, and though easy and polite in her address, she was of that inferior order of beings with regard to delicate feeling, tender sentiments, and refined sensibility, of which Augusta was one.

She stayed but half an hour, and neither in the course of her visit confided to me any of her secret thoughts, nor requested me to confide in her any of mine. You will easily imagine therefore, my dear Marianne, that I could not feel any ardent affection or very sincere attachment for Lady Dorothea.

Adieu,

Laura

LETTER THE EIGHTH
Laura to Marianne, in continuation

Lady Dorothea had not left us long before another visitor, as unexpected a one as her ladyship, was announced. It was Sir Edward who, informed by Augusta of her brother's marriage, came doubtless to reproach him for having dared to unite himself to me without his knowledge. But Edward, foreseeing his design, approached him with heroic fortitude as soon as he entered the room, and addressed him in the following manner:

'Sir Edward, I know the motive of your journey here. You come with the base design of reproaching me for having entered into an indissoluble engagement with my Laura without your consent. But, sir, I glory in the act – it is my greatest boast that I have incurred the displeasure of my father!'

So saying, he took my hand and, whilst Sir Edward, Philippa, and Augusta were doubtless reflecting with admiration on his undaunted bravery, led me from the parlour to his father's carriage which yet remained at the door, and in which we were instantly conveyed from the pursuit of Sir Edward.

The postilions had at first received orders only to take the London road; as soon as we had sufficiently reflected, however, we ordered them to drive to M**, the seat of Edward's most particular friend, which was but a few miles distant.

At M** we arrived in a few hours, and on sending in our names were immediately admitted to Sophia, the wife of Edward's friend. After having been deprived during the course of three weeks of a real friend (for such I term your mother), imagine my transports at beholding one most truly worthy of the name. Sophia was rather above the middle size; most elegantly formed. A soft languor spread over her lovely features, but increased their beauty. It was the characteristic of her mind: she was all sensibility and feeling. We flew into each others arms, and after having exchanged vows of mutual friendship for the rest of our lives, instantly unfolded to each other the most inward secrets of our hearts. We were interrupted in the delightful employment by the entrance of Augustus, Edward's friend, who was just returned from a solitary ramble.

Never did I see such an affecting scene as was the meeting of Edward and Augustus.

'My life! my soul!' exclaimed the former.

'My adorable angel!' replied the latter, as they flew into each other's arms.

It was too pathetic for the feelings of Sophia and myself – we fainted alternately on a sofa.

Adieu,

Laura

LETTER THE NINTH
From the same to the same

Towards the close of the day we received the following letter from Philippa:

> *Sir Edward is greatly incensed by your abrupt departure; he has taken back Augusta to Bedfordshire. Much as I wish to enjoy again your charming society, I cannot determine to snatch you from that of such dear and deserving friends. When your visit to them is terminated, I trust you will return to the arms of your*
>
> *Philippa*

We returned a suitable answer to this affectionate note, and after thanking her for her kind invitation, assured her that we would certainly avail ourselves of it whenever we might have no other place to go to. Though certainly nothing could, to any reasonable being, have appeared more satisfactory than so grateful a reply to her invitation, yet I know not how it was, but she was certainly capricious enough to be displeased with our behaviour, and in a few weeks after, either to revenge our conduct or relieve her own solitude, married a young and illiterate fortune-hunter. This imprudent step (though we were sensible that it would probably deprive us of that fortune which Philippa had ever taught us to expect) could not on our own accounts excite from our exalted minds a single sigh; yet fearful lest it might prove a source of endless misery to the deluded bride, our trembling sensibility was greatly affected when we were first informed of the event. The affectionate entreaties of Augustus and Sophia that we would for ever consider their house as our home easily prevailed on us to determine never more to leave them.

In the society of my Edward and this amiable pair I passed the happiest moments of my life: our time was most delightfully spent in mutual protestations of friendship and in vows of unalterable love, in which we were secure from being interrupted by intruding and disagreeable visitors as Augustus and Sophia had, on their first entrance in the neighbourhood, taken due care to inform the surrounding families that, as their happiness centred wholly in themselves, they wished for no other society.

But alas! my dear Marianne, such happiness as I then enjoyed was too perfect to be lasting. A most severe and unexpected blow at once destroyed every sensation of pleasure. Convinced as you must be, from what I have already told you concerning Augustus and Sophia, that there never were a happier couple, I need not, I imagine, inform you that their union had been contrary to the inclinations of their cruel and mercenary parents, who had vainly endeavoured with obstinate perseverance to force them into a marriage with those whom they had ever abhorred; but with a heroic fortitude worthy to be related and admired, they had both constantly refused to submit to such despotic power.

After having so nobly disentangled themselves from the shackles of parental authority by a clandestine marriage, they were determined never to forfeit the good opinion they had gained in the world in so doing by accepting any proposals of reconciliation that might be offered them by their fathers. To this further trial of their noble independence, however, they never were exposed.

They had been married but a few months when our visit to them commenced, during which time they had been amply supported by a considerable sum of money which Augustus had gracefully purloined from his unworthy father's escritoire a few days before his union with Sophia.

By our arrival their expenses were considerably increased, though their means for supplying them were then nearly exhausted. But they, exalted creatures! scorned to reflect a moment on their pecuniary distresses, and would have blushed at the idea of paying their debts. – Alas! what was their reward for such disinterested behaviour! The beautiful Augustus was arrested and we were all undone. Such perfidious treachery in the merciless perpetrators of the deed will shock your gentle nature, dearest Marianne, as much as it then affected the delicate sensibility of Edward, Sophia, your Laura, and of Augustus himself. To complete such unparalleled barbarity, we were informed that an execution in the house would shortly take place. Ah! what could we do but what we did! We sighed and fainted on the sofa.

Adieu,

Laura

LETTER THE TENTH
Laura in continuation

When we were somewhat recovered from the overpowering effusions of our grief, Edward desired that we would consider what was the most prudent step to be taken in our unhappy situation while he repaired to his imprisoned friend to lament over his misfortunes. We promised that we would, and he set forwards on his journey to town. During his absence we faithfully complied with his desire, and after the most mature deliberation, at length agreed that the best thing we could do was to leave the house, of which we every moment expected the officers of justice to take possession.

We waited therefore with the greatest impatience for the return of Edward in order to impart to him the result of our deliberations. But no Edward appeared. In vain did we count the tedious moments of his absence – in vain did we weep – in vain even did we sigh – no Edward returned –. This was too cruel, too unexpected a blow to our gentle sensibility – we could not support it – we could only faint. At length, collecting all the resolution I was mistress of, I arose and, after packing up some necessary apparel for Sophia and myself, I dragged her to a carriage I had ordered and we instantly set out for London. As the habitation of Augustus was within twelve miles of town, it was not long e'er we arrived there, and no sooner had we entered Holborn than, letting down one of the front glasses, I enquired of every decent-looking person that we passed if they had seen my Edward.

But as we drove too rapidly to allow them to answer my repeated enquiries, I gained little, or indeed, no information concerning him.

'Where am I to drive?' said the postilion.

'To Newgate, gentle youth,' replied I, 'to see Augustus.'

'Oh! no, no,' exclaimed Sophia. 'I cannot go to Newgate. I shall not be able to support the sight of my Augustus in so cruel a confinement – my feelings are sufficiently shocked by the *recital* of his distress, but to behold it will overpower my sensibility.'

As I perfectly agreed with her in the justice of her sentiments, the postilion was instantly directed to return into the country.

You may perhaps have been somewhat surprised, my dearest Marianne, that in the distress I then endured, destitute of any support, and unprovided with any habitation, I should never once have remembered my father and mother or my paternal cottage in the Vale of Usk. To account for this seeming forgetfulness I must inform you of a trifling circumstance concerning them which I have as yet never mentioned. The death of my parents a few weeks after my departure is the circumstance I allude to. By their decease I became the lawful inheritress of their house and fortune. But alas! the house had never been their own, and their fortune had only been an annuity on their own lives. Such is the depravity of the world! To your mother I should have returned with pleasure, should have been happy to have introduced to her my charming Sophia, and should, with cheerfulness, have passed the remainder of my life in their dear society in the Vale of Usk, had not one obstacle to the execution of so agreeable a scheme intervened: which was the marriage and removal of your mother to a distant part of Ireland.

Adieu,

Laura

LETTER THE ELEVENTH
Laura in continuation

'I have a relation in Scotland,' said Sophia to me as we left London, 'who I am certain would not hesitate in receiving me.'

'Shall I order the boy to drive there?' said I – but instantly recollecting myself, exclaimed, 'Alas I fear it will be too long a journey for the horses.'

Unwilling, however, to act only from my own inadequate knowledge of the strength and abilities of horses, I consulted the postilion, who was entirely of my opinion concerning the affair. We therefore determined to change horses at the next town and to travel post the remainder of the journey.

When we arrived at the last inn we were to stop at, which

was but a few miles from the house of Sophia's relation, unwilling to intrude our society on him unexpected and unthought of, we wrote a very elegant and well-penned note to him containing an account of our destitute and melancholy situation, and of our intention to spend some months with him in Scotland. As soon as we had dispatched this letter, we immediately prepared to follow it in person, and were stepping into the carriage for that purpose when our attention was attracted by the entrance of a coroneted coach and four into the inn yard. A gentleman, considerably advanced in years, descended from it. At his first appearance my sensibility was wonderfully affected and e'er I had gazed at him a second time, an instinctive sympathy whispered to my heart that he was my grandfather.

Convinced that I could not be mistaken in my conjecture, I instantly sprang from the carriage I had just entered, and, following the venerable stranger into the room he had been shown to, I threw myself on my knees before him and besought him to acknowledge me as his grandchild. He started, and having attentively examined my features, raised me from the ground and, throwing his grandfatherly arms around my neck, exclaimed, 'Acknowledge thee! Yes, dear resemblance of my Laurina and Laurina's daughter, sweet image of my Claudia and my Claudia's mother, I do acknowledge thee as the daughter of the one and the granddaughter of the other.'

While he was thus tenderly embracing me, Sophia, astonished at my precipitate departure, entered the room in search of me. No sooner had she caught the eye of the venerable peer than he exclaimed with every mark of astonishment: 'Another granddaughter! Yes, yes, I see you are the daughter of my Laurina's eldest girl; your resemblance to the beauteous Matilda sufficiently proclaims it.'

'Oh!' replied Sophia, 'when I first beheld you the instinct of nature whispered me that we were in some degree related. But whether grandfathers or grandmothers, I could not pretend to determine.'

He folded her in his arms, and whilst they were tenderly embracing, the door of the apartment opened and a most beautiful young man appeared. On perceiving him Lord St Clair started, and retreating back a few paces, with uplifted hands, said, 'Another grandchild! What an unexpected happiness is this! To discover in the space of three minutes as many of my descendants! This I am certain is Philander, the son of my Laurina's third girl, the amiable Bertha; there wants now but the presence of Gustavus to complete the union of my Laurina's grandchildren.'

'And here he is,' said a graceful youth, who that instant entered the room. 'Here is the Gustavus you desire to see. I am the son of Agatha, your Laurina's fourth and youngest daughter.'

'I see you are indeed,' replied Lord St Clair. 'But tell me,' continued he, looking fearfully towards the door, 'tell me, have I any other grandchildren in the house?'

'None, my lord.'

'Then I will provide for you all without further delay. Here are four banknotes of fifty pounds each – take them and remember I have done the duty of a grandfather.'

He instantly left the room and immediately afterwards the house.

Adieu,

Laura

You may imagine how greatly we were surprised by the sudden departure of Lord St Clair. 'Ignoble grandsire!' exclaimed Sophia; 'Unworthy grandfather!' said I, and instantly fainted in each other's arms. How long we remained in this situation I know not, but when we recovered we found ourselves alone, without either Gustavus, Philander, or the banknotes.

As we were deploring our unhappy fate, the door of the apartment opened and 'Macdonald' was announced. He was Sophia's cousin. The haste with which he came to our relief so soon after the receipt of our note spoke so greatly in his favour that I hesitated not to pronounce him, at first sight, a tender and sympathetic friend. Alas! he little deserved the name – for though he told us that he was much concerned at our misfortunes, yet by his own account it appeared that the perusal of them had neither drawn from him a single sigh, nor induced him to bestow one curse on our vindictive stars.

He told Sophia that his daughter depended on her returning with him to Macdonald Hall, and that as his cousin's friend he should be happy to see me there also. To Macdonald Hall, therefore, we went, and were received with great kindness by Janetta, the daughter of Macdonald, and the mistress of the mansion. Janetta was then only fifteen; naturally well disposed, endowed with a susceptible heart, and a sympathetic disposition, she might, had these amiable qualities been properly encouraged, have been an ornament to human nature; but unfortunately her father possessed not a soul sufficiently exalted to admire so promising a disposition, and had endeavoured by every means in his power to prevent it increasing with her years. He had actually so far extinguished the natural noble sensibility of her heart as to prevail on her to accept an offer from a young man of his recommendation. They were to be married in a few months, and Graham was in the house when we arrived. *We* soon saw through his character.

He was just such a man as one might have expected to be the choice of Macdonald. They said he was sensible, well informed, and agreeable; we did not pretend to judge of such trifles, but as we were convinced he had no soul, that he had never read the *Sorrows of Werther* [3], and that his hair bore not the least resemblance to auburn, we were certain that Janetta could feel no affection for him, or at least that she ought to feel none. The very circumstance of his being her father's choice, too, was so much in his disfavour that, had he been deserving her in every other respect, yet *that* of itself ought to have been a sufficient reason in the eyes of Janetta for rejecting him.

These considerations we were determined to represent to her in their proper light, and doubted not of meeting with the desired success from one naturally so well disposed; whose errors in the affair had only arisen from a want of proper confidence in her own opinion, and a suitable contempt of her father's. We found her, indeed, all that our warmest wishes could have hoped for; we had no difficulty to convince her that it was impossible she could love Graham, or that it was her duty to disobey her father; the only thing at which she rather seemed to hesitate was our assertion that she must be attached to some other person. For some time she persevered in declaring that she knew no other young man for whom she had the smallest affection; but upon explaining the impossibility of such a thing she said that she believed she *did like* Captain M'Kenrie better than anyone she knew besides.

This confession satisfied us and, after having enumerated the good qualities of M'Kenrie and assured her that she was violently in love with him, we desired to know whether he had ever in any wise declared his affection to her.

'So far from having ever declared it, I have no reason to imagine that he has ever felt any for me,' said Janetta.

'That he certainly adores you,' replied Sophia, 'there can be no doubt. The attachment must be reciprocal. Did he never gaze on you with admiration – tenderly press your hand – drop an involuntary tear – and leave the room abruptly?'

'Never,' replied she, 'that I remember – he has always left the room indeed when his visit has been ended, but has never gone away particularly abruptly or without making a bow.'

'Indeed, my love,' said I, 'you must be mistaken – for it is absolutely impossible that he should ever have left you but with confusion, despair, and precipitation. Consider but for a moment, Janetta, and you must be convinced how absurd it is to suppose that he could ever make a bow, or behave like any other person.'

Having settled this point to our satisfaction, the next we took into consideration was to determine in what manner we should inform M'Kenrie of the favourable opinion Janetta entertained of him. We at length agreed to acquaint him with it by an anonymous letter which Sophia drew up in the following manner:

Oh! happy lover of the beautiful Janetta; oh! amiable possessor of her heart whose hand is destined to another, why do you thus delay a confession of your attachment to the amiable object of it? Oh! consider that a few weeks will at once put an end to every flattering hope that you may now entertain, by uniting the unfortunate victim of her father's cruelty to the execrable and detested Graham.

Alas! why do you thus so cruelly connive at the projected misery of her and of yourself by delaying to communicate that scheme which had doubtless long possessed your imagination? A secret union will at once secure the felicity of both.

The amiable M'Kenrie, whose modesty as he afterwards assured us had been the only reason of his having so long concealed the violence of his affection for Janetta, on receiving this billet flew on the wings of love to Macdonald Hall, and so powerfully pleaded his attachment to her who inspired it that after a few more private interviews, Sophia and I experienced the satisfaction of seeing them depart for Gretna Green, which they chose for the celebration of their nuptials, in preference to any other place, although it was at a considerable distance from Macdonald Hall.

Adieu,

Laura

Letter The Thirteenth
Laura in continuation

They had been gone nearly a couple of hours before either Macdonald or Graham had entertained any suspicion of the affair. And they might not even then have suspected it, but for the following little accident. Sophia, happening one day to open a private drawer in Macdonald's library with one of her own keys, discovered that it was the place where he kept his papers of consequence and amongst them some banknotes of considerable amount. This discovery she imparted to me; and having agreed together that it would be a proper treatment of so vile a wretch as Macdonald to deprive him of money, perhaps dishonestly gained, it was determined that the next time we should either of us happen to go that way, we would take one or more of the banknotes from the drawer.

This well-meant plan we had often successfully put in execution; but alas! on the very day of Janetta's escape, as Sophia was majestically removing the fifth banknote from the drawer to her own purse, she was suddenly most impertinently interrupted in her employment by the entrance of Macdonald himself, in a most abrupt and precipitate manner. Sophia (who, though naturally all winning sweetness, could, when occasions demanded it, call forth the dignity of her sex) instantly put on a most forbidding look, and, darting an angry frown on the undaunted culprit, demanded in a haughty tone of voice wherefore her retirement was thus insolently broken in on.

The unblushing Macdonald, without even endeavouring to exculpate himself from the crime he was charged with, meanly endeavoured to reproach Sophia with ignobly defrauding him of his money. The dignity of Sophia was wounded.

'Wretch,' exclaimed she, hastily replacing the banknote in the drawer, 'how darest thou to accuse me of an act, of which the bare idea makes me blush?'

The base wretch was still unconvinced, and continued to upbraid the justly offended Sophia in such opprobious language that at length he so greatly provoked the gentle sweetness of her nature as to induce her to revenge herself on him by informing him of Janetta's elopement and of the active part we had both taken in the affair. At this period of their quarrel I entered the library and was, as you may imagine, equally offended as Sophia at the ill-grounded accusations of the malevolent and contemptible Macdonald.

'Base miscreant!' cried I. 'How canst thou thus undauntedly endeavour to sully the spotless reputation of such bright excellence? Why dost thou not suspect *my* innocence as soon?'

'Be satisfied, madam,' replied he, 'I *do* suspect it, and therefore must desire that you will both leave this house in less than half an hour.'

'We shall go willingly,' answered Sophia. 'Our hearts have long detested thee, and nothing but our friendship for thy daughter could have induced us to remain so long beneath thy roof.'

'Your friendship for my daughter has indeed been most powerfully exerted by throwing her into the arms of an unprincipled fortune-hunter,' replied he.

'Yes,' exclaimed I, 'amidst every misfortune, it will afford us some consolation to reflect that by this one act of friendship to Janetta, we have amply discharged every obligation that we have received from her father.'

'It must indeed be a most grateful reflection to your exalted minds,' said he.

As soon as we had packed up our wardrobe and valuables, we left Macdonald Hall, and after having walked about a mile and a half we sat down by the side of a clear limpid stream to refresh our exhausted limbs. The place was suited to meditation.

A grove of full-grown elms sheltered us from the east; a bed of full-grown nettles from the west. Before us ran the murmuring brook and behind us ran the turnpike road. We were in a mood for contemplation and in a disposition to enjoy so beautiful a spot. A mutual silence which had for some time reigned between us was at length broke by my exclaiming, 'What a lovely scene! Alas why are not Edward and Augustus here to enjoy its beauties with us?'

'Ah! my beloved Laura,' cried Sophia, 'for pity's sake forbear recalling to my remembrance the unhappy situation of my imprisoned husband. Alas, what would I not give to learn the fate of my Augustus! to know if he is still in Newgate, or if he is yet hung. But never shall I be able so far to conquer my tender sensibility as to enquire after him. Oh! do not I beseech you ever let me again hear you repeat his beloved name… It affects me too deeply… I cannot bear to hear him mentioned; it wounds my feelings.'

'Excuse me, my Sophia, for having thus unwillingly offended you,' replied I, and then, changing the conversation, desired her to admire the noble grandeur of the elms which sheltered us from the eastern zephyr.

'Alas! my Laura,' returned she, 'avoid so melancholy a subject, I entreat you. Do not again wound my sensibility by observations on those elms. They remind me of Augustus. He was like them: tall, majestic – he possessed that noble grandeur which you admire in them.'

I was silent, fearful lest I might any more unwillingly distress her by fixing on any other subject of conversation which might again remind her of Augustus.

'Why do you not speak, my Laura?' said she, after a short pause. 'I cannot support this silence – you must not leave me to my own reflections; they ever recur to Augustus.'

'What a beautiful sky!' said I. 'How charmingly is the azure varied by those delicate streaks of white!'

'Oh! my Laura,' replied she, hastily withdrawing her eyes from a momentary glance at the sky. 'Do not thus distress me by calling my attention to an object which so cruelly reminds me of my Augustus' blue satin waistcoat striped in white! In pity to your unhappy friend avoid a subject so distressing.'

What could I do? The feelings of Sophia were at that time so exquisite, and the tenderness she felt for Augustus so poignant that I had not power to start any other topic, justly fearing that it might in some unforeseen manner again awaken all her sensibility by directing her thoughts to her husband. Yet to be silent would be cruel; she had entreated me to talk.

From this dilemma I was most fortunately relieved by an accident truly apropos; it was the lucky overturning of a gentleman's phaeton on the road which ran murmuring behind us. It was a most fortunate accident as it diverted the attention of Sophia from the melancholy reflections which she had been before indulging. We instantly quitted our seats and ran to the rescue of those who, but a few moments before, had been in so elevated a situation as a fashionably high phaeton, but who were now laid low and sprawling in the dust.

'What an ample subject for reflection on the uncertain enjoyments of this world, would not that phaeton and the life of Cardinal Wolsey[4] afford a thinking mind!' said I to Sophia, as we were hastening to the field of action.

She had not time to answer me, for every thought was now engaged by the horrid spectacle before us. Two gentlemen most elegantly attired, but weltering in their blood, was what first struck our eyes – we approached – they were Edward and Augustus. Yes, dearest Marianne, they were our husbands. Sophia shrieked and fainted on the ground – I screamed and instantly ran mad –. We remained thus mutually deprived of our senses some minutes, and on regaining them were deprived of them again.

For an hour and a quarter did we continue in this unfortunate situation – Sophia fainting every moment and I running mad as often. At length a groan from the hapless Edward (who alone retained any share of life) restored us to ourselves. Had we indeed before imagined that either of them lived, we should have been more sparing of our grief, but as we had supposed when we first beheld them that they were no more, we knew that nothing could remain to be done but what we were about.

No sooner, therefore, did we hear my Edward's groan than, postponing our lamentations for the present, we hastily ran to the dear youth and, kneeling on each side of him, implored him not to die.

'Laura,' said he, fixing his now languid eyes on me. 'I fear I have been overturned.'

I was overjoyed to find him yet sensible.

'Oh! tell me Edward,' said I, 'tell me, I beseech you before you die, what has befallen you since that unhappy day in which Augustus was arrested and we were separated.'

'I will,' said he, and instantly fetching a deep sigh, expired.

Sophia immediately sank again into a swoon – *my* grief was more audible. My voice faltered, my eyes assumed a vacant stare, my face became as pale as death, and my senses were considerably impaired.

'Talk not to me of phaetons,' said I, raving in a frantic, incoherent manner. 'Give me a violin – I'll play to him and soothe him in his melancholy hours – beware, ye gentle nymphs, of Cupid's thunderbolts, avoid the piercing shafts of Jupiter – look at that grove of firs – I see a leg of mutton – they told me Edward was not dead; but they deceived me – they took him for a cucumber –' Thus I continued, wildly exclaiming on my Edward's death.

For two hours did I rave thus madly and should not then have left off, as I was not in the least fatigued, had not Sophia, who was just recovered from her swoon, entreated me to consider that night was now approaching and that the damps began to fall.

'And whither shall we go,' said I, 'to shelter us from either?'

'To that white cottage,' replied she, pointing to a neat building which rose up amidst the grove of elms and which I had not before observed. I agreed, and we instantly walked to it. We knocked at the door – it was opened by an old woman; on being requested to afford us a night's lodging, she informed us that her house was but small, that she had only two bedrooms, but that however, we should be welcome to one of them. We were satisfied and followed the good woman into the house where we were greatly cheered by the sight of a comfortable fire. She was a widow and had only one daughter who was then just seventeen – one of the best of ages; but alas! she was very plain and her name was Bridget... Nothing therefore could be expected from her – she could not be supposed to possess either exalted ideas, delicate feelings or refined sensibilities. She was nothing more than a mere good-tempered, civil and obliging young woman; as such we could scarcely dislike her – she was only an object of contempt.

Adieu,

Laura

LETTER THE FOURTEENTH
Laura in continuation

Arm yourself, my amiable young friend, with all the philosophy you are mistress of; summon up all the fortitude you possess, for alas! in the perusal of the following pages your sensibility will be most severely tried. Ah! what were the misfortunes I had before experienced and which I have already related to you, to the one I am now going to inform you of. The death of my father, my mother and my husband, though almost more than my gentle nature could support, were trifles in comparison to the misfortune I am now proceeding to relate.

The morning after our arrival at the cottage, Sophia complained of a violent pain in her delicate limbs, accompanied with a disagreeable headache. She attributed it to a cold caught by her continued faintings in the open air as the dew was falling the evening before. This I feared was but too probably the case; since how could it be otherwise accounted for that I should have escaped the same indisposition, but by supposing that the bodily exertions I had undergone in my repeated fits of frenzy had so effectually circulated and warmed my blood as to make me proof against the chilling damps of night, whereas Sophia, lying totally inactive on the ground, must have been exposed to all their severity. I was most seriously alarmed by her illness which, trifling as it may appear to you, a certain instinctive sensibility whispered me would in the end be fatal to her.

Alas! my fears were but too fully justified; she grew gradually worse – and I daily became more alarmed for her. At length she was obliged to confine herself solely to the bed allotted us by our worthy landlady.

Her disorder turned to a galloping consumption, and in a few days carried her off. Amidst all my lamentations for her (and violent you may suppose they were) I yet received some consolation in the reflection of my having paid every attention to her that could be offered in her illness. I had wept over her every day – had bathed her sweet face with my tears, and had pressed her fair hands continually in mine.

'My beloved Laura,' said she to me, a few hours before she died, 'take warning from my unhappy end and avoid the imprudent conduct which has occasioned it… Beware of fainting fits… Though at the time they may be refreshing and agreeable, yet believe me, they will, in the end, if too often repeated and at improper seasons, prove destructive to your constitution… My fate will teach you this… I die a martyr to my grief for the loss of Augustus… One fatal swoon has cost me my life… Beware of swoons, dear Laura… A frenzy fit is not one quarter so pernicious; it is an exercise to the body and, if not too violent, is, I dare say, conducive to health in its consequences. Run mad as often as you choose; but do not faint.'

These were the last words she ever addressed to me. It was her dying advice to her afflicted Laura, who has ever most faithfully adhered to it.

After having attended my lamented friend to her early grave, I immediately (though late at night) left the detested village in which she died, and near which had expired my husband and Augustus. I had not walked many yards from it before I was overtaken by a stagecoach, in which I instantly took a place, determined to proceed in it to Edinburgh, where I hoped to find some kind, pitying friend who would receive and comfort me in my afflictions.

It was so dark when I entered the coach that I could not distinguish the number of my fellow-travellers; I could only perceive that they were many. Regardless, however, of anything concerning them, I gave myself up to my own sad reflections. A general silence prevailed – a silence which was by nothing interrupted but by the loud and repeated snores of one of the party.

'What an illiterate villain must that man be!' thought I to myself. 'What a total want of delicate refinement must he have, who can thus shock our senses by such a brutal noise! He must, I am certain, be capable of every bad action! There is no crime too black for such a character!' Thus reasoned I within myself, and doubtless such were the reflections of my fellow-travellers.

At length, returning day enabled me to behold the unprincipled scoundrel who had so violently disturbed my feelings. It was Sir Edward, the father of my deceased husband. By his side sat Augusta, and on the same seat with me were your mother and Lady Dorothea. Imagine my surprise at finding myself thus seated amongst my old acquaintance. Great as was my astonishment, it was yet increased when, on looking out of windows, I beheld the husband of Philippa, with Philippa by his side, on the coach-box, and when, on looking behind, I beheld Philander and Gustavus in the basket.

'Oh! Heavens,' exclaimed I, 'is it possible that I should so unexpectedly be surrounded by my nearest relations and connections?' These words roused the rest of the party, and every eye was directed to the corner in which I sat.

'Oh! my Isabel,' continued I, throwing myself across Lady Dorothea into her arms, 'receive once more to your bosom the unfortunate Laura. Alas! when we last parted in the Vale of Usk, I was happy in being united to the best of Edwards; I had then a father and a mother, and had never known misfortunes. But now, deprived of every friend but you –'

'What!' interrupted Augusta. 'Is my brother dead then? Tell us I entreat you what is become of him?'

'Yes, cold and insensible nymph,' replied I, 'that luckless swain, your brother, is no more, and you may now glory in being the heiress of Sir Edward's fortune.'

Although I had always despised her from the day I had overheard her conversation with my Edward, yet in civility I complied with hers and Sir Edward's entreaties that I would inform them of the whole melancholy affair. They were greatly shocked – even the obdurate heart of Sir Edward and the insensible one of Augusta were touched with sorrow by the unhappy tale. At the request of your mother I related to them every other misfortune which had befallen me since we parted. Of the imprisonment of Augustus and the absence of Edward – of our arrival in Scotland – of our unexpected meeting with our grandfather and our cousins – of our visit to Macdonald Hall – of the singular service we there performed towards Janetta – of her father's ingratitude for it – of his inhuman behaviour, unaccountable suspicions, and barbarous treatment of us in obliging us to leave the house – of our lamentations on the loss of Edward and Augustus, and finally of the melancholy death of my beloved companion.

Pity and surprise were strongly depictured in your mother's countenance during the whole of my narration, but I am sorry to say that, to the eternal reproach of her sensibility, the latter infinitely predominated. Nay, faultless as my conduct had certainly been during the whole course of my late misfortunes and adventures, she pretended to find fault with my behaviour in many of the situations in which I had been placed. As I was sensible myself that I had always behaved in a manner which reflected honour on my feelings and refinement, I paid little attention to what she said, and desired her to satisfy my curiosity by informing me how she came there, instead of wounding my spotless reputation with unjustifiable reproaches. As soon as she had complied with my wishes in this particular and had given me an accurate detail of everything that had befallen her since our separation (the particulars of which, if you are not already acquainted with, your mother will give you), I applied to Augusta for the same information respecting herself, Sir Edward and Lady Dorothea.

She told me that, having a considerable taste for the beauties of nature, her curiosity to behold the delightful scenes it exhibited in that part of the world had been so much raised by Gilpin's tour to the Highlands[5] that she had prevailed on her father to undertake a tour to Scotland, and had persuaded Lady Dorothea to accompany them. That they had arrived at Edinburgh a few days before and from thence had made daily excursions into the country around in the stagecoach they were then in, from one of which excursions they were at that time returning.

My next enquiries were concerning Philippa and her husband, the latter of whom I learnt, having spent all her fortune, had recourse for subsistence to the talent in which he had always most excelled, namely, driving; and that having sold everything which belonged to them except their coach, had converted it into a stage and, in order to be removed from any of his former acquaintance, had driven it to Edinburgh, from whence he went to Stirling every other day; that Philippa, still retaining her affection for her ungrateful husband, had followed him to Scotland and generally accompanied him in his little excursions to Stirling.

'It has only been to throw a little money into their pockets,' continued Augusta, 'that my father has always travelled in their coach to view the beauties of the country since our arrival in Scotland – for it would certainly have been much more agreeable to us to visit the Highlands in a post-chaise than merely to travel from Edinburgh to Stirling, and from Stirling to Edinburgh every other day in a crowded and uncomfortable stage.' I perfectly agreed with her in her sentiments on the affair, and secretly blamed Sir Edward for thus sacrificing his daughter's pleasure for the sake of a ridiculous old woman whose folly in marrying so young a man ought to be punished. His behaviour, however, was entirely of a piece with his general character; for what could be expected from a man who possessed not the smallest atom of sensibility, who scarcely knew the meaning of sympathy, and who actually snored –

Adieu,

Laura

Letter The Fifteenth
Laura in continuation

When we arrived at the town where we were to breakfast, I was determined to speak with Philander and Gustavus, and to that purpose as soon as I left the carriage, I went to the basket and tenderly enquired after their health, expressing my fears of the uneasiness of their situation. At first they seemed rather confused at my appearance, dreading, no doubt, that I might call them to account for the money which our grandfather had left me and which they had unjustly deprived me of, but finding that I mentioned nothing of the matter, they desired me to step into the basket as we might there converse with greater ease. Accordingly I entered and, whilst the rest of the party were devouring green tea and buttered toast, we feasted ourselves in a more refined and sentimental manner by a confidential conversation. I informed them of everything which had befallen me during the course of my life, and at my request they related to me every incident of theirs.

'We are the sons, as you already know, of the two youngest daughters which Lord St Clair had by Laurina, an Italian opera-girl. Our mothers could neither of them exactly ascertain who were our fathers, though it is generally believed that Philander is the son of one Philip Jones, a bricklayer, and that my father was one Gregory Staves, a stay-maker of Edinburgh. This is, however, of little consequence for, as our mothers were certainly never married to either of them, it reflects no dishonour on our blood, which is of a most ancient and unpolluted kind.

'Bertha, the mother of Philander, and Agatha, my own mother, always lived together. They were neither of them very rich; their united fortunes had originally amounted to nine thousand pounds, but as they had always lived on the principal of it, when we were fifteen it was diminished to nine hundred. This nine hundred they always kept in a drawer in one of the tables which stood in our common sitting parlour, for the convenience of having it always at hand. Whether it was from this circumstance, of its being easily taken, or from a wish of being independent, or from an excess of sensibility (for which we were always remarkable) I cannot now determine, but certain it is that when we had reached our fifteenth year, we took the nine hundred pounds and ran away. Having obtained this prize we were determined to manage it with economy and not to spend it either with folly or extravagance. To this purpose we therefore divided it into nine parcels, one of which we devoted to victuals, the second to drink, the third to housekeeping, the fourth to carriages, the fifth to horses, the sixth to servants, the seventh to amusements, the eighth to clothes, and the ninth to silver buckles.

Having thus arranged our expenses for two months (for we expected to make the nine hundred pounds last as long), we hastened to London and had the good luck to spend it in seven weeks and a day, which was six days sooner than we had intended. As soon as we had thus happily disencumbered ourselves from the weight of so much money, we began to think of returning to our mothers, but, accidentally hearing that they were both starved to death, we gave over the design and determined to engage ourselves to some strolling company of players, as we had always a turn for the stage. Accordingly we offered our services to one and were accepted; our company was indeed rather small, as it consisted only of the manager, his wife and ourselves, but there were fewer to pay and the only inconvenience attending it was the scarcity of plays which, for want of people to fill the characters, we could perform.

We did not mind trifles however. One of our most admired performances was *Macbeth*, in which we were truly great. The manager always played Banquo himself, his wife my Lady Macbeth. I did the Three Witches, and Philander all the rest. To say the truth, this tragedy was not only the best, but the only play that we ever performed; and after having acted it all over England and Wales, we came to Scotland to exhibit it over the remainder of Great Britain. We happened to be quartered in that very town where you came and met your grandfather.

We were in the inn yard when his carriage entered and, perceiving by the arms to whom it belonged, and knowing that Lord St Clair was our grandfather, we agreed to endeavour to get something from him by discovering the relationship. You know how well it succeeded. Having obtained the two hundred pounds, we instantly left the town, leaving our manager and his wife to act *Macbeth* by themselves, and took the road to Stirling, where we spent our little fortune with great éclat. We are now returning to Edinburgh in order to get some preferment in the acting way; and such, my dear cousin, is our history.'

I thanked the amiable youth for his entertaining narration, and after expressing my wishes for their welfare and happiness, left them in their little habitation and returned to my other friends who impatiently expected me.

My adventures are now drawing to a close, my dearest Marianne; at least for the present.

When we arrived at Edinburgh Sir Edward told me that as the widow of his son, he desired I would accept from his hands of four hundred a year. I graciously promised that I would, but could not help observing that the unsympathetic baronet offered it more on account of my being the widow of Edward than in being the refined and amiable Laura.

I took up my residence in a romantic village in the Highlands of Scotland, where I have ever since continued, and where I can, uninterrupted by unmeaning visits, indulge in a melancholy solitude, my unceasing lamentations for the death of my father, my mother, my husband and my friend.

Augusta has been for several years united to Graham, the man of all others most suited to her; she became acquainted with him during her stay in Scotland.

Sir Edward, in hopes of gaining an heir to his title and estate, at the same time married Lady Dorothea. His wishes have been answered.

Philander and Gustavus, after having raised their reputation by their performances in the theatrical line at Edinburgh, removed to Covent Garden, where they still exhibit under the assumed names of Lewis and Quick.

Philippa has long paid the debt of nature; her husband, however, still continues to drive the stagecoach from Edinburgh to Stirling.

Adieu, my dearest Marianne.

Laura

The Three Sisters

To Edward Austen[1] *Esq.,*
the following unfinished novel is respectfully inscribed by
his obedient humble servant,
the author

Miss Stanhope to Mrs **

My dear Fanny,

I am the happiest creature in the world, for I have received an offer of marriage from Mr Watts. It is the first I have ever had, and I hardly know how to value it enough. How I will triumph over the Duttons! I do not intend to accept it, at least I believe not, but as I am not quite certain I gave him an equivocal answer and left him. And now, my dear Fanny, I want your advice whether I should accept his offer or not, but that you may be able to judge of his merits and the situation of affairs I will give you an account of them.

He is quite an old man, about two and thirty, very plain – so plain that I cannot bear to look at him. He is extremely disagreeable and I hate him more than anybody else in the world. He has a large fortune and will make great settlements on me; but then he is very healthy. In short I do not know what to do. If I refuse him he as good as told me that he should offer himself to Sophia, and if she refused him, to Georgiana, and I could not bear to have either of them married before me. If I accept him I know I shall be miserable all the rest of my life, for he is very ill tempered and peevish, extremely jealous, and so stingy that there is no living in the house with him. He told me he should mention the affair to Mamma, but I insisted upon it that he did not, for very likely she would make me marry him whether I would or no; however probably he *has* before now, for he never does anything he is desired to do. I believe I shall have him. It will be such a triumph to be married before Sophy, Georgiana, and the Duttons; and he promised to have a new carriage on the occasion, but we almost quarrelled about the colour, for I insisted upon its being blue spotted with silver, and he declared it should be a plain chocolate; and to provoke me more, said it should be just as low as his old. I won't have him, I declare. He said he should come again tomorrow and take my final answer, so I believe I must get him while I can. I know the Duttons will envy me and I shall be able to chaperone Sophy and Georgiana to all the winter balls. But then what will be the use of that when very likely he won't let me go myself, for I know he hates dancing, and what he hates himself he has no idea of any other person's liking; and besides he talks a great deal of women's always staying at home and such stuff. I believe I shan't have him; I would refuse him at once if I were certain that neither of my sisters would accept him, and that if they did not, he would not offer to the Duttons. I cannot run such a risk, so, if he will promise to have the carriage ordered as I like, I will have him; if not he may ride in it by himself for me. I hope you like my determination; I can think of nothing better; and am your ever affectionate

Mary Stanhope

From the same to the same

Dear Fanny,

I had but just sealed my last letter to you when my mother came up and told me she wanted to speak to me on a very particular subject.

'Ah! I know what you mean,' said I. 'That old fool Mr Watts has told you all about it, though I bid him not. However you shan't force me to have him if I don't like it.'

'I am not going to force you, child, but only want to know what your resolution is with regard to his proposals, and to insist upon your making up your mind one way or t'other, that if you don't accept him Sophy may.'

'Indeed,' replied I, hastily. 'Sophy need not trouble herself for I shall certainly marry him myself.'

'If that is your resolution,' said my mother, 'why should you be afraid of my forcing your inclinations?'

'Why, because I have not settled whether I shall have him or not.'

'You are the strangest girl in the world, Mary. What you say one moment, you unsay the next. Do tell me once for all whether you intend to marry Mr Watts or not?'

'Law, Mamma, how can I tell you what I don't know myself?'

'Then I desire you will know, and quickly too, for Mr Watts says he won't be kept in suspense.'

'That depends upon me.'

'No it does not, for if you do not give him your final answer tomorrow when he drinks tea with us, he intends to pay his addresses to Sophy.'

'Then I shall tell all the world that he behaved very ill to me.'

'What good will that do? Mr Watts has been too long abused by all the world to mind it now.'

'I wish I had a father or a brother because then they should fight him.'

'They would be cunning if they did, for Mr Watts would run away first; and therefore you must and shall resolve either to accept or refuse him before tomorrow evening.'

'But why if I don't have him, must he offer to my sisters?'

'Why! because he wishes to be allied to the family, and because they are as pretty as you are.'

'But will Sophy marry him, Mamma, if he offers to her?'

'Most likely. Why should not she? If, however, she does not choose it, then Georgiana must, for I am determined not to let such an opportunity escape of settling one of my daughters so advantageously. So, make the most of your time; I leave you to settle the matter with yourself.' And then she went away.

The only thing I can think of, my dear Fanny, is to ask Sophy and Georgiana whether they would have him were he to make proposals to them, and if they say they would not, I am resolved to refuse him too, for I hate him more than you can imagine. As for the Duttons, if he marries one of them I shall still have the triumph of having refused him first.

So, adieu my dear friend –

Yours ever,

M.S.

Miss Georgiana Stanhope to Miss **

Wednesday

My dear Anne,

Sophy and I have just been practising a little deceit on our eldest sister, to which we are not perfectly reconciled, and yet the circumstances were such that if anything will excuse it, they must.

Our neighbour Mr Watts has made proposals to Mary; proposals which she knew not how to receive, for though she has a particular dislike to him (in which she is not singular), yet she would willingly marry him sooner than risk his offering to Sophy or me which, in case of a refusal from herself, he told her he should do, for you must know the poor girl considers our marrying before her as one of the greatest misfortunes that can possibly befall her, and to prevent it would willingly ensure herself everlasting misery by a marriage with Mr Watts.

An hour ago she came to us to sound our inclinations respecting the affair which were to determine hers. A little before she came, my mother had given us an account of it, telling us that she certainly would not let him go further than our own family for a wife. 'And therefore,' said she, 'if Mary won't have him Sophy must, and if Sophy won't Georgiana *shall*.' Poor Georgiana! We neither of us attempted to alter my mother's resolution, which, I am sorry to say, is generally more strictly kept than rationally formed. As soon as she was gone, however, I broke silence to assure Sophy that if Mary should refuse Mr Watts I should not expect her to sacrifice her happiness by becoming his wife from a motive of generosity to me, which I was afraid her good nature and sisterly affection might induce her to do.

'Let us flatter ourselves,' replied she, 'that Mary will not refuse him. Yet how can I hope that my sister may accept a man who cannot make her happy.'

'*He* cannot, it is true, but his fortune, his name, his house, his carriage will, and I have no doubt but that Mary will marry him; indeed why should she not? He is not more than two and thirty; a very proper age for a man to marry at; he is rather plain to be sure, but then what is beauty in a man; if he has but a genteel figure and a sensible looking face it is quite sufficient.'

'This is all very true, Georgiana, but Mr Watts's figure is unfortunately extremely vulgar and his countenance is very heavy.'

'And then as to his temper, it has been reckoned bad, but may not the world be deceived in their judgement of it. There is an open frankness in his disposition which becomes a man. They say he is stingy; we'll call that prudence. They say he is suspicious; that proceeds from a warmth of heart always excusable in youth, and in short I see no reason why he should not make a very good husband, or why Mary should not be very happy with him.'

Sophy laughed.

I continued, 'However, whether Mary accepts him or not, I am resolved. My determination is made. I never would marry Mr Watts were beggary the only alternative. So deficient in every respect! Hideous in his person and without one good quality to make amends for it. His fortune to be sure is good. Yet not so very large! Three thousand a year. What is three thousand a year? It is but six times as much as my mother's income. It will not tempt me.'

'Yet it will be a noble fortune for Mary,' said Sophy, laughing again.

'For Mary! Yes indeed it will give me pleasure to see her in such affluence.'

Thus I ran on to the great entertainment of my sister till Mary came into the room to appearance in great agitation. She sat down. We made room for her at the fire. She seemed at a loss how to begin and at last said, in some confusion:

'Pray, Sophy, have you any mind to be married?'

'To be married! None in the least. But why do you ask me? Are you acquainted with anyone who means to make me proposals?'

'I – no, how should I? But mayn't I ask a common question?'

'Not a very common one, Mary, surely,' said I. She paused, and after some moments silence went on:

'How should you like to marry Mr Watts, Sophy?'

I winked at Sophy and replied for her. 'Who is there but must rejoice to marry a man of three thousand a year?'

'Very true,' she replied. 'That's very true. So you would have him if he would offer, Georgiana, and would you Sophy?'

Sophy did not like the idea of telling a lie and deceiving her sister; she prevented the first and saved half her conscience by equivocation.

'I should certainly act just as Georgiana would do.'

'Well then,' said Mary, with triumph in her eyes, 'I have had an offer from Mr Watts.'

We were of course very much surprised.

'Oh! do not accept him,' said I, 'and then perhaps he may have me.'

In short my scheme took, and Mary is resolved to do that to prevent our supposed happiness which she would not have done to ensure it in reality. Yet, after all, my heart cannot acquit me, and Sophy is even more scrupulous.

Quiet our minds, my dear Anne, by writing and telling us you approve our conduct. Consider it well over. Mary will have real pleasure in being a married woman, and able to chaperone us, which she certainly shall do, for I think myself bound to contribute as much as possible to her happiness in a state I have made her choose. They will probably have a new carriage, which will be paradise to her, and if we can prevail on Mr W. to set up his phaeton she will be too happy. These things however would be no consolation to Sophy or me for domestic misery. Remember all this and do not condemn us.

Friday

Last night Mr Watts, by appointment, drank tea with us. As soon as his carriage stopped at the door, Mary went to the window.

'Would you believe it, Sophy,' said she, 'the old fool wants to have his new chaise just the colour of the old one, and hung as low too. But it shan't – I *will* carry my point. And if he won't let it be as high as the Duttons', and blue spotted with silver, I won't have him. Yes I will too. Here he comes. I know he'll be rude; I know he'll be ill-tempered and won't say one civil thing to me! nor behave at all like a lover.' She then sat down and Mr Watts entered.

'Ladies, your most obedient.' We paid our compliments and he seated himself.

'Fine weather, ladies.' Then turning to Mary: 'Well, Miss Stanhope, I hope you have at last settled the matter in your own mind, and will be so good as to let me know whether you will condescend to marry me or not.'

'I think, sir,' said Mary, 'you might have asked in a genteeler way than that. I do not know whether I *shall* have you if you behave so odd.'

'Mary!' said my mother.

'Well, Mamma, if he will be so cross –'

'Hush, hush, Mary, you shall not be rude to Mr Watts.'

'Pray, madam, do not lay any restraint on Miss Stanhope by obliging her to be civil. If she does not choose to accept my hand, I can offer it elsewhere, for as I am by no means guided by a particular preference to you above your sisters. It is equally the same to me which I marry of the three.'

Was there ever such a wretch! Sophy reddened with anger and I felt so spiteful!

'Well then,' said Mary, in a peevish accent, 'I *will* have you if I *must*.'

'I should have thought, Miss Stanhope, that when such settlements are offered as I have offered to you, there can be no great violence done to the inclinations in accepting of them.'

Mary mumbled out something, which I who sat close to her could just distinguish to be: 'What's the use of a great jointure if men live for ever?' And then audibly: 'Remember the pin money[2]; two hundred a year.'

'A hundred and seventy-five, madam.'

'Two hundred indeed, sir,' said my mother.

'And remember I am to have a new carriage hung as high as the Duttons', and blue spotted with silver; and I shall expect a new saddle horse, a suit of fine lace, and an infinite number of the most valuable jewels. Diamonds such as never were seen! and pearls, rubies, emeralds, and beads out of number. You must set up your phaeton, which must be cream coloured with a wreath of silver flowers round it. You must buy four of the finest bays in the kingdom and you must drive me in it every day. This is not all. You must entirely new furnish your house after my taste. You must hire two more footmen to attend me, two women to wait on me, must always let me do just as I please, and make a very good husband.'

Here she stopped, I believe rather out of breath.

'This is all very reasonable, Mr Watts, for my daughter to expect.'

'And it is very reasonable, Mrs Stanhope, that your daughter should be disappointed.' He was going on but Mary interrupted him.

'You must build me an elegant greenhouse and stock it with plants. You must let me spend every winter in Bath, every spring in town, every summer in taking some tour, and every autumn at a watering place, and if we are at home the rest of the year' – Sophy and I laughed – 'you must do nothing but give balls and masquerades. You must build a room on purpose and a theatre to act plays in. The first play we have shall be *Which is the Man*[3], and I will do Lady Bell Bloomer.'

'And pray, Miss Stanhope,' said Mr Watts, 'what am I to expect from you in return for all this?'

'Expect? Why, you may expect to have me pleased.'

'It would be odd if I did not. Your expectations, madam, are too high for me, and I must apply to Miss Sophy, who perhaps may not have raised hers so much.'

'You are mistaken, sir, in supposing so,' said Sophy. 'For though they may not be exactly in the same line, yet my expectations are to the full as high as my sister's, for I expect my husband to be good-tempered and cheerful, to consult my happiness in all his actions, and to love me with constancy and sincerity.'

Mr Watts stared. 'These are very odd ideas truly, young lady. You had better discard them before you marry, or you will be obliged to do it afterwards.'

My mother, in the meantime, was lecturing Mary who was sensible that she had gone too far, and when Mr Watts was just turning towards me in order, I believe, to address me, she spoke to him in a voice half humble, half sulky.

'You are mistaken, Mr Watts, if you think I was in earnest when I said I expected so much. However I must have a new chaise.'

'Yes, sir, you must allow that Mary has a right to expect that.'

'Mrs Stanhope, I *mean* and have always meant to have a new one on my marriage. But it shall be the colour of my present one.'

'I think, Mr Watts, you should pay my girl the compliment of consulting her taste on such matters.'

Mr Watts would not agree to this, and for some time insisted upon its being a chocolate colour, while Mary was as eager for having it blue with silver spots. At length, however, Sophy proposed that to please Mr W. it should be a dark brown, and to please Mary it should be hung rather high and have a silver border. This was at length agreed to, though reluctantly on both sides, as each had intended to carry their point entire.

We then proceeded to other matters, and it was settled that they should be married as soon as the writings could be completed. Mary was very eager for a special licence and Mr

Watts talked of banns. A common licence was at last agreed on. Mary is to have all the family jewels, which are very inconsiderable I believe, and Mr W. promised to buy her a saddle horse, but in return she is not to expect to go to town or any other public place for these three years. She is to have neither greenhouse, theatre or phaeton; to be contented with one maid, without an additional footman. It engrossed the whole evening to settle these affairs; Mr W. supped with us and did not go till twelve.

As soon as he was gone Mary exclaimed, 'Thank Heaven! he's off at last; how I do hate him!' It was in vain that Mamma represented to her the impropriety she was guilty of in disliking him who was to be her husband, for she persisted in declaring her aversion to him and hoping she might never see him again. What a wedding will this be!

Adieu, my dear Anne.

Your faithfully sincere

Georgiana Stanhope

From the same to the same

Saturday

Dear Anne,

Mary, eager to have everyone know of her approaching wedding, and more particularly desirous of triumphing, as she called it, over the Duttons, desired us to walk with her this morning to Stoneham. As we had nothing else to do we readily agreed, and had as pleasant a walk as we could have with Mary whose conversation entirely consisted in abusing the man she is soon to marry and in longing for a blue chaise spotted with silver. When we reached the Duttons' we found the two girls in the dressing room with a very handsome young man, who was of course introduced to us. He is the son of Sir Henry Brudenell of Leicestershire. Mr Brudenell is the handsomest man I ever saw in my life; we are all three very much pleased with him. Mary, who from the moment of our reaching the dressing room had been swelling with the knowledge of her own importance and with the desire of making it known, could not remain long silent on the subject after we were seated, and soon addressing herself to Kitty said, 'Don't you think it will be necessary to have all the jewels new set?'

'Necessary for what?'

'For what! Why for my appearance.'

'I beg your pardon, but I really do not understand you. What jewels do you speak of, and where is your appearance to be made?'

'At the next ball to be sure, after I am married.'

You may imagine their surprise. They were at first incredulous, but on our joining in the story they at last believed it. 'And who is it to?' was of course the first question. Mary pretended bashfulness, and answered in confusion, her eyes cast down, 'To Mr Watts.' This also required confirmation from us, for that anyone who had the beauty and fortune (though small, yet a provision) of Mary would willingly marry Mr Watts, could by them scarcely be credited. The subject being now fairly introduced, and she found herself the object of everyone's attention in company, she lost all her confusion and became perfectly unreserved and communicative.

'I wonder you should never have heard of it before, for in general things of this nature are very well known in the neighbourhood.'

'I assure you,' said Jemima, 'I never had the least suspicion of such an affair. Has it been in agitation long?'

'Oh! yes, ever since Wednesday.'

54

They all smiled, particularly Mr Brudenell.

'You must know Mr Watts is very much in love with me, so that it is quite a match of affection on his side.'

'Not on his only, I suppose,' said Kitty.

'Oh! when there is so much love on one side, there is no occasion for it on the other. However I do not much dislike him, though he is very plain to be sure.'

Mr Brudenell stared, the Miss Duttons laughed, and Sophy and I were heartily ashamed of our sister. She went on.

'We are to have a new post-chaise and very likely may set up our phaeton.'

This we knew to be false, but the poor girl was pleased at the idea of persuading the company that such a thing was to be, and I would not deprive her of so harmless an enjoyment. She continued.

'Mr Watts is to present me with the family jewels which I fancy are very considerable.'

I could not help whispering Sophy, 'I fancy not.'

'These jewels are what I suppose must be new set before they can be worn. I shall not wear them till the first ball I go to after my marriage. If Mrs Dutton should not go to it, I hope you will let me chaperone you; I shall certainly take Sophy and Georgiana.'

'You are very good,' said Kitty, 'and since you are inclined to undertake the care of young ladies, I should advise you to prevail on Mrs Edgecumbe to let you chaperone her six daughters which, with your two sisters and ourselves, will make your entrée very respectable.'

Kitty made us all smile, except Mary who did not understand her meaning and coolly said that she should not like to chaperone so many. Sophy and I now endeavoured to change the conversation but succeeded only for a few minutes, for

Mary took care to bring back their attention to her and her approaching wedding. I was sorry for my sister's sake to see that Mr Brudenell seemed to take pleasure in listening to her account of it, and even encouraged her by his questions and remarks, for it was evident that his only aim was to laugh at her. I am afraid he found her very ridiculous. He kept his countenance extremely well, yet it was easy to see that it was with difficulty he kept it. At length, however, he seemed fatigued and disgusted with her ridiculous conversation, as he turned from her to us, and spoke but little to her for about half an hour before we left Stoneham. As soon as we were out of the house we all joined in praising the person and manners of Mr Brudenell.

We found Mr Watts at home.

'So, Miss Stanhope,' said he, 'you see I am come a-courting in a true lover-like manner.'

'Well, you need not have *told* me that. I knew why you came very well.'

Sophy and I then left the room, imagining of course that we must be in the way if a scene of courtship were to begin. We were surprised at being followed almost immediately by Mary.

'And is your courting so soon over?' said Sophy.

'Courting!' replied Mary. 'We have been quarrelling. Watts is such a fool! I hope I shall never see him again.'

'I am afraid you will,' said I, 'as he dines here today. But what has been your dispute?'

'Why, only because I told him that I had seen a man much handsomer than he was this morning, he flew into a great passion and called me a vixen, so I only stayed to tell him I thought him a blackguard and came away.'

'Short and sweet,' said Sophy, 'but pray, Mary, how will this be made up?'

'He ought to ask my pardon; but if he did, I would not forgive him.'

'His submission then would not be very useful.'

When we were dressed we returned to the parlour where Mamma and Mr Watts were in close conversation. It seems that he had been complaining to her of her daughter's behaviour, and she had persuaded him to think no more of it. He therefore met Mary with all his accustomed civility, and except one touch at the phaeton and another at the greenhouse, the evening went off with a great harmony and cordiality. Watts is going to town to hasten the preparations for the wedding.

I am your affectionate friend

G.S.

A Collection of Letters

To Miss Cooper
Cousin,
Conscious of the charming character which in every country and every clime in Christendom is cried, concerning you, with caution and care I commend to your charitable criticism this clever collection of curious comments, which have been carefully culled, collected and classed by your comical cousin, the author

LETTER THE FIRST
From a Mother to Her Friend

My children begin now to claim all my attention in a different manner from that in which they have been used to receive it, as they are now arrived at that age when it is necessary for them, in some measure, to become conversant with the world. My Augusta is seventeen and her sister scarcely a twelvemonth younger. I flatter myself that their education has been such as will not disgrace their appearance in the world, and that *they* will not disgrace their education I have every reason to believe. Indeed, they are sweet girls: sensible yet unaffected; accomplished yet easy; lively yet gentle.

As their progress in everything they have learnt has been always the same, I am willing to forget the difference of age, and to introduce them together into public. This very evening is fixed on as their first entrée into life, as we are to drink tea with Mrs Cope and her daughter. I am glad that we are to meet no one for my girls' sake, as it would be awkward for them to enter too wide a circle on the very first day. But we shall proceed by degrees –. Tomorrow Mr Stanly's family will drink tea with us, and perhaps the Miss Phillips will meet them. On Tuesday we shall pay morning visits; on Wednesday we are to dine at Westbrook. On Thursday we have company at home. On Friday we are to be at a private concert at Sir John Wynna's; and on Saturday we expect Miss Dawson to call in the morning, which will complete my daughters' introduction into life. How they will bear so much dissipation I cannot imagine; of their spirits I have no fear, I only dread their health.

This mighty affair is now happily over, and my girls are *out*. As the moment approached for our departure, you can have no idea how the sweet creatures trembled with fear and expectation. Before the carriage drove to the door, I called them into my dressing room, and as soon as they were seated, thus addressed them.

'My dear girls, the moment is now arrived when I am to reap the rewards of all my anxieties and labours towards you during your education. You are this evening to enter a world in which you will meet with many wonderful things; yet let me warn you against suffering yourselves to be meanly swayed by the follies and vices of others, for believe me, my beloved children, that if you do, I shall be very sorry for it.' They both assured me that they would ever remember my advice with gratitude, and follow it with attention; that they were prepared to find a world full of things to amaze and to shock them, but that they trusted their behaviour would never give me reason to repent the watchful care with which I had presided over their infancy and formed their minds –

'With such expectations and such intentions,' cried I, 'I can have nothing to fear from you – and can cheerfully conduct you to Mrs Cope's without a fear of your being seduced by her example, or contaminated by her follies. Come, then, my children,' added I, 'the carriage is driving to the door, and I will not a moment delay the happiness you are so impatient to enjoy.'

When we arrived at Warleigh, poor Augusta could scarcely breathe, while Margaret was all life and rapture.

'The long-expected moment is now arrived,' said she, 'and we shall soon be in the world.'

In a few moments we were in Mrs Cope's parlour, where with her daughter she sat ready to receive us. I observed with delight the impression my children made on them –. They were indeed two sweet, elegant-looking girls, and though somewhat abashed from the peculiarity of their situation, yet there was an ease in their manners and address which could not fail of pleasing –. Imagine, my dear madam, how delighted I must have been in beholding, as I did, how attentively they observed every object they saw, how disgusted with some things, how enchanted with others, how astonished at all! On the whole, however, they returned in raptures with the world, its inhabitants, and manners.

Yours ever,

A.F.

Letter the Second
From a Young Lady Crossed in Love to Her Friend

Why should this last disappointment hang so heavily on my spirits? Why should I feel it more, why should it wound me deeper than those I have experienced before? Can it be that I have a greater affection for Willoughby than I had for his amiable predecessors? Or is it that our feelings become more acute from being often wounded? I must suppose, my dear Belle, that this is the case, since I am not conscious of being more sincerely attached to Willoughby than I was to Neville, Fitzowen, or either of the Crawfords, for all of whom I once felt the most lasting affection that ever warmed a woman's heart. Tell me then, dear Belle, why I still sigh when I think of the faithless Edward, or why I weep when I behold his bride, for too surely this is the case –. My friends are all alarmed for me; they fear my declining health; they lament my want of spirits; they dread the effects of both. In hopes of relieving my melancholy, by directing my thoughts to other objects, they have invited several of their friends to spend the Christmas with us. Lady Bridget Dashwood and her sister-in-law, Miss Jane, are expected on Friday; and Colonel Seaton's family will be with us next week. This is all most kindly meant by my uncle and cousins, but what can the presence of a dozen indifferent people do to me, but weary and distress me? I will not finish my letter till some of our visitors are arrived.

Friday evening

Lady Bridget came this morning, and, with her, her sweet sister Miss Jane. Although I have been acquainted with this charming woman above fifteen years, yet I never before observed how lovely she is. She is now about thirty-five, and in spite of sickness, sorrow and time, is more blooming than I ever saw a girl of seventeen. I was delighted with her the moment she entered the house, and she appeared equally pleased with me, attaching herself to me during the remainder of the day. There is something so sweet, so mild in her countenance that she seems more than mortal. Her conversation is as bewitching as her appearance; I could not help telling her how much she engaged my admiration. 'Oh! Miss Jane,' said I – and stopped from an inability, at the moment, of expressing myself as I could wish – 'Oh! Miss Jane,' I repeated – I could not think of words to suit my feelings –. She seemed waiting for my speech –. I was confused – distressed – my thoughts were bewildered – and I could only add – 'How do you do?'

She saw and felt for my embarrassment, and with admirable presence of mind, relieved me from it by saying: 'My dear Sophia, be not uneasy at having exposed yourself – I will turn the conversation without appearing to notice it.' Oh! how I loved her for her kindness! 'Do you ride as much as you used to do?' said she.

'I am advised to ride by my physician. We have delightful rides round us, I have a charming horse, am uncommonly fond of the amusement,' replied I, quite recovered from my confusion, 'and in short I ride a great deal.'

'You are in the right, my love,' said she. Then, repeating the following line which was an extempore and equally adapted to recommend both riding and candour: 'Ride where you may; be candid where you can,' she added: 'I rode once, but it is many years ago –' She spoke this in so low and tremulous a voice that I was silent – struck with her manner of speaking, I could make no reply. 'I have not ridden,' continued she, fixing her eyes on my face, 'since I was married.' I was never so surprised –. 'Married, ma'am!' I repeated. 'You may well wear that look of astonishment,' said she, 'since what I have said must appear improbable to you. Yet nothing is more true than that I once was married.'

'Then why are you called Miss Jane?'

'I married, my Sophia, without the consent or knowledge of my father, the late Admiral Annesley. It was therefore necessary to keep the secret from him and from everyone till some fortunate opportunity might offer of revealing it –. Such an opportunity alas! was but too soon given in the death of my dear Captain Dashwood –. Pardon these tears,' continued Miss Jane, wiping her eyes, 'I owe them to my husband's memory. He fell, my Sophia, while fighting for his country in America after a most happy union of seven years –. My children, two sweet boys and a girl, who had constantly resided with my father and me, passing with him and with everyone as the children of a brother (though I had ever been an only child) had as yet been the comforts of my life. But no sooner had I lost my Henry than these sweet creatures fell sick and died –. Conceive, dear Sophia, what my feelings must have been when, as an aunt, I attended my children to their early grave –. My father did not survive them many weeks – he died, poor good old man, happily ignorant to his last hour of my marriage.'

'But did not you own it, and assume his name at your husband's death?'

'No; I could not bring myself to do it; more especially when in my children I lost all inducement for doing it. Lady Bridget and yourself are the only persons who are in the knowledge of my having ever been either wife or mother. As I could not prevail on myself to take the name of Dashwood – a name which, after my Henry's death, I could never hear without emotion – and as I was conscious of having no right to that of Annesley, I dropped all thoughts of either, and have made it a point of bearing only my Christian one since my father's death.' She paused.

'Oh! my dear Miss Jane,' said I, 'how infinitely am I obliged to you for so entertaining a story! You cannot think how it has diverted me! But have you quite done?'

'I have only to add, my dear Sophia, that my Henry's elder brother dying about the same time, Lady Bridget became a widow like myself, and as we had always loved each other in idea from the high character in which we had ever been spoken of, though we had never met, we determined to live together. We wrote to one another on the same subject by the same post, so exactly did our feeling and our actions coincide! We both eagerly embraced the proposals we gave and received of becoming one family, and have from that time lived together in the greatest affection.'

'And is this all? said I, 'I hope you have not done.'

'Indeed I have; and did you ever hear a story more pathetic?'

'I never did – and it is for that reason it pleases me so much, for when one is unhappy nothing is so delightful to one's sensations as to hear of equal misery.'

'Ah! but my Sophia why are *you* unhappy?'

'Have you not heard, madam, of Willoughby's marriage?'

'But, my love, why lament *his* perfidy when you bore so well that of many young men before?'

'Ah! madam, I was used to it then, but when Willoughby broke his engagements I had not been disappointed for half a year.'

'Poor girl!' said Miss Jane.

LETTER THE THIRD
From a Young Lady in Distressed Circumstances to Her Friend

A few days ago I was at a private ball given by Mr Ashburnham. As my mother never goes out she entrusted me to the care of Lady Greville, who did me the honour of calling for me in her way and of allowing me to sit forwards, which is a favour about which I am very indifferent, especially as I know it is considered as conferring a great obligation on me.

'So Miss Maria,' said her ladyship, as she saw me advancing to the door of the carriage, 'you seem very smart tonight – *my* poor girls will appear quite to disadvantage by *you*. I only hope your mother may not have distressed herself to set *you* off. Have you got a new gown on?'

'Yes ma'am,' replied I, with as much indifference as I could assume.

'Aye, and a fine one too, I think,' feeling it, as by her permission I seated myself by her. 'I dare say it is all very smart – but I must own, for you know I always speak my mind, that I think it was quite a needless piece of expense – why could not you have worn your old striped one? It is not my way to find fault with people because they are poor, for I always think that they are more to be despised and pitied than blamed for it, especially if they cannot help it. But at the same time I must say that in my opinion your old striped gown would have been quite fine enough for its wearer, for to tell you the truth – I always speak my mind – I am very much afraid that one half of the people in the room will not know whether you have a gown on or not –. But I suppose you intend to make your fortune tonight. Well, the sooner the better; and I wish you success.'

'Indeed, ma'am, I have no such intention –'

'Whoever heard a young lady own that she was a fortune-hunter?'

Miss Greville laughed, but I am sure Ellen felt for me.

'Was your mother gone to bed before you left her?' said her ladyship.

'Dear ma'am,' said Ellen, 'it is but nine o'clock.'

'True Ellen, but candles cost money, and Mrs Williams is too wise to be extravagant.'

'She was just sitting down to supper, ma'am.'

'And what had she got for supper?'

'I did not observe.'

'Bread and cheese I suppose.'

'I should never wish for a better supper,' said Ellen.

'You have never any reason,' replied her mother, 'as a better is always provided for you.' Miss Greville laughed excessively, as she constantly does at her mother's wit.

Such is the humiliating situation in which I am forced to appear while riding in her ladyship's coach. I dare not be impertinent, as my mother is always admonishing me to be humble and patient if I wish to make my way in the world. She insists on my accepting every invitation of Lady Greville, or you may be certain that I would never enter either her house, or her coach, with the disagreeable certainty I always have of being abused for my poverty while I am in them.

When we arrived at Ashburnham, it was nearly ten o'clock, which was an hour and a half later than we were desired to be there, but Lady Greville is too fashionable – or fancies herself to be so – to be punctual. The dancing, however, was not begun as they waited for Miss Greville. I had not been long in the room before I was engaged to dance by Mr Bernard, but just as we were going to stand up, he recollected that his servant had got his white gloves, and immediately ran out to fetch them. In the meantime the dancing began and Lady Greville, in passing to another room, went exactly before me. She saw me and, instantly stopping, said to me, though there were several people close to us, 'Hey day, Miss Maria! What, cannot you get a partner? Poor young lady! I am afraid your new gown was put on for nothing. But do not despair, perhaps you may get a hop before the evening is over.'

So saying, she passed on without hearing my repeated assurance of being engaged, and leaving me very much provoked at being so exposed before everyone. Mr Bernard, however, soon returned and, by coming to me the moment he entered the room and leading me to the dancers, my character, I hope, was cleared from the imputation Lady Greville had thrown on it in the eyes of all the old ladies who had heard her speech. I soon forgot all my vexations in the pleasure of dancing and of having the most agreeable partner in the room. As he is, moreover, heir to a very large estate, I could see that Lady Greville did not look very well pleased when she found who had been his choice.

She was determined to mortify me, and accordingly, when we were sitting down between the dances, she came to me with more than her usual insulting importance, attended by Miss Mason, and said, loud enough to be heard by half the people in the room, 'Pray Miss Maria, in what way of business was your grandfather? for Miss Mason and I cannot agree whether he was a grocer or a bookbinder.' I saw that she wanted to mortify me, and was resolved if I possibly could to prevent her seeing that her scheme succeeded.

'Neither, madam; he was a wine merchant.'

'Aye, I knew he was in some such low way – he broke, did not he?'

'I believe not, ma'am.'

'Did not he abscond?'

'I never heard that he did.'

'At least he died insolvent?'

'I was never told so before.'

'Why, was not your *father* as poor as a rat?'

'I fancy not.'

'Was not he in the King's Bench once?'

'I never saw him there.'

She gave me *such* a look, and turned away in a great passion; while I was half delighted with myself for my impertinence, and half afraid of being thought too saucy.

As Lady Greville was extremely angry with me, she took no further notice of me all the evening, and indeed, had I been in favour, I should have been equally neglected, as she was got into a party of great folks and she never speaks to me when she can to anyone else. Miss Greville was with her mother's party at supper, but Ellen preferred staying with the Bernards and me. We had a very pleasant dance and, as Lady G. slept all the way home, I had a very comfortable ride.

The next day, while we were at dinner, Lady Greville's coach stopped at the door, for that is the time of day she generally contrives it should. She sent in a message by the servant to say that 'she should not get out but that Miss Maria must come to the coach door as she wanted to speak to her, and that she must make haste and come immediately –'

'What an impertinent message, Mamma!' said I.

'Go Maria,' replied she. Accordingly I went and was obliged to stand there at her ladyship's pleasure, though the wind was extremely high and very cold.

'Why, I think, Miss Maria, you are not quite so smart as you were last night. But I did not come to examine your dress, but

to tell you that you may dine with us the day after tomorrow –
not tomorrow, remember, do not come tomorrow, for we
expect Lord and Lady Clermont and Sir Thomas Stanley's
family. There will be no occasion for your being very fine for
I shan't send the carriage – if it rains you may take an umbrella'
– I could hardly help laughing at hearing her give me leave to
keep myself dry – 'and pray remember to be on time, for I
shan't wait – I hate my victuals overdone. But you need not
come *before* the time –. How does your mother do? She is at
dinner is not she?'

'Yes, ma'am, we were in the middle of dinner when your
ladyship came.'

'I am afraid you find it very cold Maria,' said Ellen.

'Yes, it is a horrible east wind,' said her mother. 'I assure you
I can hardly bear the window down. But you are used to be
blown about by the wind, Miss Maria, and that is what has
made your complexion so ruddy and coarse. You young ladies
who cannot often ride in a carriage never mind what weather
you trudge in, or how the wind shows your legs. I would not
have *my* girls stand out of doors as you do in such a day as this.
But some sort of people have no feelings either of cold or
delicacy –. Well, remember that we shall expect you on
Thursday at five o'clock. You must tell your maid to come for
you at night –. There will be no moon, and you will have a
horrid walk home.

'My compliments to your mother – I am afraid your dinner
will be cold – drive on –' And away she went, leaving me in a
great passion with her as she always does.

Maria Williams

LETTER THE FOURTH
From a Young Lady Rather Impertinent to Her Friend

We dined yesterday with Mr Evelyn where we were introduced to a very agreeable-looking girl, his cousin. I was extremely pleased with her appearance, for added to the charms of an engaging face, her manner and voice had something peculiarly interesting in them. So much so that they inspired me with a great curiosity to know the history of her life, who were her parents, where she came from, and what had befallen her, for it was then only known that she was a relation of Mr Evelyn, and that her name was Grenville. In the evening a favourable opportunity offered to me of attempting at least to know what I wished to know, for everyone played at cards but Mrs Evelyn, my mother, Dr Drayton, Miss Grenville and myself, and as the two former were engaged in a whispering conversation, and the doctor fell asleep, we were of necessity obliged to entertain each other. This was what I wished, and being determined not to remain in ignorance for want of asking, I began the conversation in the following manner.

'Have you been long in Essex, ma'am?'

'I arrived on Tuesday.'

'You came from Derbyshire?'

'No, ma'am!' appearing surprised at my question, 'from Suffolk.'

You will think this a good dash of mine, my dear Mary, but you know that I am not wanting for impudence when I have any end in view. 'Are you pleased with the country, Miss Grenville? Do you find it equal to the one you have left?'

'Much superior, ma'am, in point of beauty.' She sighed.

I longed to know for why.

'But the face of any country, however beautiful,' said I, 'can be but a poor consolation for the loss of one's dearest friends.' She shook her head, as if she felt the truth of what I said. My curiosity was so much raised that I was resolved at any rate to satisfy it.

'You regret having left Suffolk then, Miss Grenville?'

'Indeed I do.'

'You were born there, I suppose?'

'Yes, ma'am, I was, and passed many happy years there –'

'That is a great comfort,' said I. 'I hope, ma'am, that you never spent any *un*happy ones there.'

'Perfect felicity is not the property of mortals, and no one has a right to expect uninterrupted happiness. – *Some* misfortunes I have certainly met with.'

'*What* misfortunes, dear ma'am?' replied I, burning with impatience to know everything.

'*None*, ma'am, I hope, that have been the effect of any wilful fault in me.'

'I dare say not, ma'am, and have no doubt but that any sufferings you may have experienced could arise only from the cruelties of relations or the errors of friends.'

She sighed.

'You seem unhappy, my dear Miss Grenville. Is it in my power to soften your misfortunes?'

'*Your* power, ma'am,' replied she, extremely surprised; 'it is in *no one's* power to make me happy.' She pronounced these words in so mournful and solemn an accent that for some time I had not courage to reply. I was actually silenced.

I recovered myself, however, in a few moments and, looking at her with all the affection I could, 'My dear Miss Grenville,' said I, 'you appear extremely young – and may probably stand in need of someone's advice whose regard for you, joined to superior age, perhaps superior judgement, might authorise her to give it. I am that person, and I now challenge you to accept the offer I make you of my confidence and friendship, in return to which I shall only ask for yours –'

'You are extremely obliging, ma'am,' said she, 'and I am highly flattered by your attention to me. But I am in no difficulty, no doubt, no uncertainty of situation in which any advice can be wanted. Whenever I am, however,' continued she, brightening into a complaisant smile, 'I shall know where to apply.'

I bowed, but felt a good deal mortified by such a repulse; still, however, I had not given up my point. I found that by the appearance of sentiment and friendship nothing was to be gained, and determined, therefore, to renew my attacks by questions and suppositions. 'Do you intend staying long in this part of England, Miss Grenville?'

'Yes, ma'am, some time I believe.'

'But how will Mr and Mrs Grenville bear your absence?'

'They are neither of them alive, ma'am.'

This was an answer I did not expect – I was quite silenced, and never felt so awkward in my life.

Letter The Fifth
From a Young Lady Very Much in Love to Her Friend

My uncle gets more stingy, my aunt more particular, and I more in love every day. What shall we all be at this rate by the end of the year! I had this morning the happiness of receiving the following letter from my dear Musgrove.

Sackville Street, January 7th
It is a month today since I first beheld my lovely Henrietta, and the sacred anniversary must, and shall, be kept in a manner becoming the day – by writing to her. Never shall I forget the moment when her beauties first broke on my sight – no time, as you well know, can erase it from my memory. It was at Lady Scudamore's. Happy Lady Scudamore to live within a mile of the divine Henrietta! When the lovely creature first entered the room, oh! what were my sensations? The sight of you was like the sight of a wonderful fine thing. I started – I gazed at her with admiration – she appeared every moment more charming, and the unfortunate Musgrove became a captive to your charms before I had time to look about me. Yes, madam, I had the happiness of adoring you, a happiness for which I cannot be too grateful. 'What!' said he to himself. 'Is Musgrove allowed to die for Henrietta?' Enviable Mortal! and may he pine for her who is the object of universal admiration, who is adored by a colonel, and toasted by a baronet! Adorable Henrietta, how beautiful you are! I declare you are quite divine! You are more than mortal. You are an angel. You are Venus herself. In short, madam, you are the prettiest girl I ever saw in my life – and her

beauty is increased in her Musgrove's eyes by permitting him to love her, and allowing me to hope. And ah! angelic Miss Henrietta, Heaven is my witness how ardently I do hope for the death of your villainous uncle and his abandoned wife, since my fair one will not consent to be mine till their decease has placed her in affluence above what my fortune can procure. Though it is an improvable estate –.

Cruel Henrietta to persist in such a resolution! I am at present with my sister where I mean to continue till my own house which, though an excellent one is at present somewhat out of repair, is ready to receive me. Amiable princess of my heart, farewell – of that heart which trembles while it signs itself –

Your most ardent admirer and devoted humble servant,

T. Musgrove

There is a pattern for a love letter, Matilda! Did you ever read such a masterpiece of writing? Such sense, such sentiment, such purity of thought, such flow of language and such unfeigned love in one sheet? No, never I can answer for it, since a Musgrove is not to be met with by every girl. Oh! how I long to be with him! I intend to send him the following in answer to his letter tomorrow.

My dearest Musgrove,

Words cannot express how happy your letter made me; I thought I should have cried for joy, for I love you better than anybody in the world. I think you the most amiable, and the handsomest man in England, and so to be sure you are. I never read so sweet a letter in my life. Do write me another just like it, and tell me you are in love with me in every other line. I quite die to see you. How shall we manage to see one another? for we are so much in love that we cannot live asunder. Oh! my dear Musgrove, you cannot think how impatiently I wait for the death of my uncle and aunt. If they will not die soon, I believe I shall run mad, for I get more in love with you every day of my life.

How happy your sister is to enjoy the pleasure of your company in her house, and how happy everybody in London must be because you are there. I hope you will be so kind as to write to me again soon, for I never read such sweet letters as yours.

I am, my dearest Musgrove, most truly and faithfully yours for ever and ever

Henrietta Halton

I hope he will like my answer; it is as good a one as I can write though nothing to his. Indeed I had always heard what a dab he was at a love letter. I saw him, you know, for the first time at Lady Scudamore's. And when I saw her ladyship afterwards she asked me how I liked her cousin Musgrove.

'Why upon my word,' said I, 'I think he is a very handsome young man.'

'I am glad you think so,' replied she, 'for he is distractedly in love with you.'

'Law! Lady Scudamore,' said I. 'How can you talk so ridiculously?'

'Nay, 'tis very true,' answered she, 'I assure you, for he was in love with you from the first moment he beheld you.'

'I wish it may be true,' said I, 'for that is the only kind of love I would give a farthing for. There is some sense in being in love at first sight.'

'Well, I give you joy of your conquest,' replied Lady Scudamore, 'and I believe it to have been a very complete one;

I am sure it is not a contemptible one, for my cousin is a charming young fellow, has seen a great deal of the world, and writes the best love letters I ever read.'

This made me very happy, and I was excessively pleased with my conquest. However, I thought it was proper to give myself a few airs, so I said to her: 'This is all very pretty, Lady Scudamore, but you know that we young ladies who are heiresses must not throw ourselves away upon men who have no fortune at all.'

'My dear Miss Halton,' said she, 'I am as much convinced of that as you can be, and I do assure you that I should be the last person to encourage your marrying anyone who had not some pretensions to expect a fortune with you. Mr Musgrove is so far from being poor that he has an estate of several hundreds a year which is capable of great improvement, and an excellent house, though at present it is not quite in repair.'

'If that is the case,' replied I, 'I have nothing more to say against him, and if, as you say, he is an informed young man and can write a good love letter, I am sure I have no reason to find fault with him for admiring me; though perhaps I may not marry him for all that, Lady Scudamore.'

'You are certainly under no obligation to marry him,' answered her ladyship, 'except that which love himself will dictate to you, for if I am not greatly mistaken you are at this very moment, unknown to yourself, cherishing a most tender affection for him.'

'Law, Lady Scudamore,' replied I, blushing. 'How can you think of such a thing?'

'Because every look, every word betrays it,' answered she. 'Come, my dear Henrietta, consider me as a friend, and be sincere with me – do not you prefer Mr Musgrove to any man of your acquaintance?'

'Pray do not ask me such questions, Lady Scudamore,' said I, turning away my head, 'for it is not fit for me to answer them.'

'Nay, my love,' replied she, 'now you confirm my suspicions. But why, Henrietta, should you be ashamed to own a well-placed love, or why refuse to confide in me?'

'I am not ashamed to own it,' said I, taking courage. 'I do not refuse to confide in you, or blush to say that I do love your cousin Mr Musgrove, that I am sincerely attached to him, for it is no disgrace to love a handsome man. If he were plain, indeed I might have had reason to be ashamed of a passion which must have been mean since the object would have been unworthy. But with such a figure and face, and such beautiful hair as your cousin has, why should I blush to own that such superior merit has made an impression on me.'

'My sweet girl,' said Lady Scudamore, embracing me with great affection, 'what a delicate way of thinking you have in these matters, and what a quick discernment for one of your years! Oh! how I honour you for such noble sentiments!'

'Do you, ma'am,' said I. 'You are vastly obliging. But pray, Lady Scudamore, did your cousin himself tell you of his affection for me? I shall like him the better if he did, for what is a lover without a confidante?'

'Oh! my love,' replied she, 'you were born for each other. Every word you say more deeply convinces me that your minds are actuated by the invisible power of sympathy, for your opinions and sentiments so exactly coincide. Nay, the colour of your hair is not very different. Yes, my dear girl, the poor despairing Musgrove did reveal to me the story of his love. Nor was I surprised at it – I know not how it was, but I had a kind of presentiment that he would be in love with you.'

'Well, but how did he break it to you?'

'It was not till after supper. We were sitting round the fire together, talking on indifferent subjects, though to say the truth, the conversation was chiefly on my side for he was thoughtful and silent, when on a sudden he interrupted me in the midst of something I was saying, by exclaiming in a most theatrical tone:

"Yes, I'm in love, I feel it now.
And Henrietta Halton has undone me!"'

'Oh! What a sweet way,' replied I, 'of declaring his passion! To make such a couple of charming lines about me! What a pity it is that they are not in rhyme!'

'I am very glad you like it,' answered she. 'To be sure there was a great deal of taste in it. "And are you in love with her, cousin?" said I. "I am very sorry for it, for unexceptionable as you are in every respect, with a pretty estate capable of great improvements, and an excellent house, though somewhat out of repair, yet who can hope to aspire with success to the adorable Henrietta who has had an offer from a colonel and been toasted by a baronet."'

'*That* I have,' cried I.

Lady Scudamore continued: ' "Ah, dear cousin," replied he, "I am so well convinced of the little chance I can have of winning her who is adored by thousands, that I need no assurances of yours to make me more thoroughly so. Yet surely neither you nor the fair Henrietta herself will deny me the exquisite gratification of dying for her, of falling a victim to her charms. And when I am dead –" 'continued her –

'Oh Lady Scudamore,' said I, wiping my eyes, 'that such a sweet creature should talk of dying!'

'It is an affecting circumstance indeed,' replied Lady Scudamore.

' "When I am dead," said he, "let me be carried and lain at her feet, and perhaps she may not disdain to drop a pitying tear on my poor remains." '

'Dear Lady Scudamore,' interrupted I, 'say no more on this affecting subject. I cannot bear it.'

'Oh! how I admire the sweet sensibility of your soul, and as I would not for worlds wound it too deeply, I will be silent.'

'Pray go on,' said I. She did so.

'And then added he: "Ah! Cousin, imagine what my transports will be when I feel the dear precious drops trickle on my face! Who would not die to taste such ecstasy! And when I am interred, may the divine Henrietta bless some happier youth with her affection; may he be as tenderly attached to her as the hapless Musgrove; and while *he* crumbles to dust, may they live an example of felicity in the conjugal state!" '

Did you ever hear anything so pathetic? What a charming wish, to be lain at my feet when he was dead! Oh! what an exalted mind he must have to be capable of such a wish! Lady Scudamore went on.

' "Ah! my dear cousin," replied I to him, "such noble behaviour as this must melt the heart of any woman, however obdurate it may naturally be; and could the divine Henrietta but hear your generous wishes for her happiness, all gentle as is her mind, I have not a doubt but that she would pity your affection and endeavour to return it." "Oh! Cousin," answered he, "do not endeavour to raise my hopes by such flattering assurances. No, I cannot hope to please this angel of a woman, and the only thing which remains for me to do, is to die." "True love is ever desponding," replied I, "but I, my dear

Tom, will give you even greater hopes of conquering this fair one's heart than I have yet given you, by assuring you that I watched her with the strictest attention during the whole day, and could plainly discover that she cherishes in her bosom, though unknown to herself, a most tender affection for you." '

'Dear Lady Scudamore,' cried I; 'this is more than I ever knew!'

'Did not I say that it was unknown to yourself? "I did not," continued I to him, "encourage you by saying this at first, that surprise might render the pleasure still greater." "No, cousin," replied he, in a languid voice, "nothing will convince me that I can have touched the heart of Henrietta Halton, and if you are deceived yourself, do not attempt deceiving me." In short, my love, it was the work of some hours for me to persuade the poor despairing youth that you had really a preference for him; but when at last he could no longer deny the force of my arguments, or discredit what I told him, his transports, his raptures, his ecstasies are beyond my power to describe.'

'Oh! the dear creature,' cried I, 'how passionately he loves me! But, dear Lady Scudamore, did you tell him that I was totally dependent on my uncle and aunt?'

'Yes, I told him everything.'

'And what did he say?'

'He exclaimed with virulence against uncles and aunts; accused the laws of England for allowing them to possess their estates when wanted by their nephews or nieces, and wished *he* were in the House of Commons, that he might reform the legislature, and rectify all its abuses.'

'Oh! the sweet man! What a spirit he has!' said I.

'He could not flatter himself, he added, that the adorable Henrietta would condescend for his sake to resign those luxuries and that splendour to which she had been used, and accept only in exchange the comforts and elegancies which his limited income could afford her, even supposing that his house were in readiness to receive her. I told him that it could not be expected that she would; it would be doing her an injustice to suppose her capable of giving up the power she now possesses and so nobly uses of doing such extensive good to the poorer part of her fellow creatures, merely for the gratification of you and herself.'

'To be sure,' said I, 'I *am* very charitable every now and then. And what did Mr Musgrove say to this?'

'He replied that he was under a melancholy necessity of owning the truth of what I said, and that therefore if he should be the happy creature destined to be the husband of the beautiful Henrietta, he must bring himself to wait, however impatiently, for the fortunate day when she might be freed from the power of worthless relations and able to bestow herself on him.'

What a noble creature he is! Oh! Matilda, what a fortunate one I am, who am to be his wife! My aunt is calling me to come and make the pies, so adieu my dear friend, and believe me yours etc. –

H. Halton

NOTES

LOVE AND FRIENDSHIP

1. Eliza de Feuillide (1761–1813) was Jane Austen's cousin.

2. In Shakespeare's *Cymbeline*, Polydore is the name adopted by Guiderius whilst in the Welsh forest.

3. Goethe's *The Sorrows of Young Werther* was first published in 1774, some sixteen years before Austen wrote *Love and Friendship*.

4. Thomas Wolsey (*c.*1475–1530) rose to become an extremely powerful cardinal and archbishop under Henry VIII before he fell from favour; his life was recounted in the remarkable biography *The Life and Death of Cardinal Wolsey* by George Cavendish (*c.*1499–*c.*1561).

5. William Gilpin's *Observations on several parts of Great Britain, particularly the High-lands of Scotland, relative chiefly to picturesque beauty, made in the year 1776* was first published in 1789, the year before *Love and Friendship* was written.

THE THREE SISTERS

1. Edward Austen (1767–1852) was Jane Austen's elder brother.

2. 'Pin-money' was the sum a husband allotted his wife for the purchase of clothes and other necessities.

3. *Which is the Man* is a sentimental comedy by Hannah Cowley (1743–1809), first performed in 1782.

Jane Austen was born in 1775 in Steventon, Hampshire, the seventh of eight children. Her father, the Revd George Austen, was a well-read and cultured man, and Jane was mostly educated at home. She read voraciously as a child, in particular the works of Fielding, Sterne, Richardson and Scott. She also began writing at a very young age, producing *Love and Friendship* when she was only fourteen. *A History of England* followed when she was sixteen, and *A Collection of Letters* at seventeen.

Following her father's death in 1805, she and her mother moved to Southampton, before settling in Chawton, Hampshire, in 1819, and it was here that her major novels were written. Despite leading a remarkably uneventful life herself – she never married, and seldom left home – her works are noted for her incredible powers of observation. Only four novels were published during her lifetime – *Sense and Sensibility* (1811), *Pride and Prejudice* (1813), *Mansfield Park* (1814) and *Emma* (1816) – and all were published anonymously. On a rare visit from home, she was taken ill, and she died from Addison's disease in 1817. Two further novels, *Persuasion* and *Northanger Abbey*, were published posthumously in 1818. *Sanditon*, the novel she was working on when she died, appeared in 1925.

HESPERUS PRESS CLASSICS

Hesperus Press, as suggested by the Latin motto, is committed to bringing near what is far – far both in space and time. Works written by the greatest authors, and unjustly neglected or simply little known in the English-speaking world, are made accessible through new translations and a completely fresh editorial approach. Through these classic works, the reader is introduced to the greatest writers from all times and all cultures.

For more information on Hesperus Press, please visit our website: **www.hesperuspress.com**

ET REMOTISSIMA PROPE

SELECTED TITLES FROM HESPERUS PRESS

Author	Title	Foreword writer
Pietro Aretino	*The School of Whoredom*	Paul Bailey
Pietro Aretino	*The Secret Life of Nuns*	
Jane Austen	*Lady Susan*	
Jane Austen	*Lesley Castle*	Zoë Heller
Honoré de Balzac	*Colonel Chabert*	A.N. Wilson
Charles Baudelaire	*On Wine and Hashish*	Margaret Drabble
Giovanni Boccaccio	*Life of Dante*	A.N. Wilson
Charlotte Brontë	*The Spell*	
Emily Brontë	*Poems of Solitude*	Helen Dunmore
Mikhail Bulgakov	*Fatal Eggs*	Doris Lessing
Mikhail Bulgakov	*The Heart of a Dog*	A.S. Byatt
Giacomo Casanova	*The Duel*	Tim Parks
Miguel de Cervantes	*The Dialogue of the Dogs*	Ben Okri
Geoffrey Chaucer	*The Parliament of Birds*	
Anton Chekhov	*The Story of a Nobody*	Louis de Bernières
Anton Chekhov	*Three Years*	William Fiennes
Wilkie Collins	*The Frozen Deep*	
Joseph Conrad	*Heart of Darkness*	A.N. Wilson
Joseph Conrad	*The Return*	Colm Tóibín
Gabriele D'Annunzio	*The Book of the Virgins*	Tim Parks
Dante Alighieri	*The Divine Comedy: Inferno*	
Dante Alighieri	*New Life*	Louis de Bernières
Daniel Defoe	*The King of Pirates*	Peter Ackroyd
Marquis de Sade	*Incest*	Janet Street-Porter
Charles Dickens	*The Haunted House*	Peter Ackroyd
Charles Dickens	*A House to Let*	
Fyodor Dostoevsky	*The Double*	Jeremy Dyson
Fyodor Dostoevsky	*Poor People*	Charlotte Hobson
Alexandre Dumas	*One Thousand and One Ghosts*